'I know you didn't believe me when I said I fell in love with you, Eliza. But it's true.

'I want to change your mind. I ask you to give me one more chance at winning the woman I will love for ever. Be my bride, here, on Saturday, in front of the whole town and all your friends. They all think we belong together, as I do, and I've asked them to help me sway you. Will you let it happen? Marry me, Eliza May, please.'

A mother to five sons, **Fiona McArthur** is an Australian midwife who loves to write. Medical Romance™ gives Fiona the scope to write about all the wonderful aspects of adventure, romance, medicine and midwifery that she feels so passionate about— as well as an excuse to travel! So, now that the boys are older, her husband Ian and youngest son Rory are off with Fiona to meet new people, see new places, and have wonderful adventures. Fiona's web site is at fionamcarthur.com

Recent titles by the same author:

DANGEROUS ASSIGNMENT
A VERY SINGLE MIDWIFE
THE PREGNANT MIDWIFE

THE DOCTOR'S SURPRISE BRIDE

BY
FIONA McARTHUR

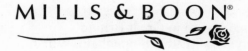

TO LISA—ALWAYS THERE WHEN I LOST FAITH

First published in Great Britain 2006
Large Print edition 2006
Harlequin Mills & Boon Limited,
Eton House, 18-24 Paradise Road,
Richmond, Surrey TW9 1SR

© Fiona McArthur 2006

ISBN-13: 978 0 263 18888 2
ISBN-10:   0 263 18888 4

Set in Times Roman 17½ on 21¾ pt.
17-1006-46909

Printed and bound in Great Britain
by Antony Rowe Ltd, Chippenham, Wiltshire

CHAPTER ONE

'ARE you OK?' Dr Jack Dancer, Medical Director—in fact, only doctor at Bellbrook Hospital—tilted his head. He tried to bring together this city woman's list of qualifications and experience—then reconcile it with her youth and the tiny package she came in. Actually, Eliza May looked like a garden fairy with attitude. Her shoulders were tense, her head tilted and she glowered fiercely at him through slitted eyes.

This woman looked ten years too young to qualify for half of her résumé and, with Mary going, the hospital needed every skill this city woman was supposed to have.

He'd thought his cousin's agency recommendation extraordinarily glowing and he wondered what fanciful planet his cousin had been on when she'd recommended this woman.

'I'm fine.' Her voice was not loud but contained an element of self-confidence that made him look at her again. She straightened and the movement added a desperately needed few centimetres to her height. Now he could see her eyes.

Jack felt a ripple shimmer down his back and his breath stuck somewhere behind suddenly sensitive ribs.

Good grief. Her eyes were amazing—vibrant green, alluring eyes that dared him to step out of line and taste the consequences. Even the jagged gold circles around her pupils seemed to glow and shimmer and draw him in. He couldn't look away.

Jack forced his diaphragm back into action, and dragged his gaze lower to accelerate past memorable lips and a determined little chin, but knew he was in trouble when he skimmed too low and had to bounce his attention out of her tightly restrained cleavage. What on earth had got into him?

'Lead on, Dr Dancer.' Now she was decisive and he felt the earth shift again under his feet. No fluttery fairy here. He quietened his reservations—and his libido. Energy vibrated and the new Eliza May held such promise for Bellbrook Hospital that he would never risk jeopardising her suitability with unwanted attention.

Perish the thought.

Whatever shock wave had belted him was past now and he wouldn't think like that again.

Realistically they had no one else, and apparently she was multi-skilled and dynamic, though a bit of a chameleon. Still, they all required diversity when Bellbrook bestowed some of those moments of unusual interest and everything went haywire.

He had a full waiting room in his surgery at the side of the hospital and his sister-in-law, Mary, had been due to start maternity leave a month ago. His cousin *had* said Eliza was reliable.

'Right, then.' He didn't look at her again. 'As soon as we find our matron, she'll show you around. I won't see you until later when I do my evening round at the hospital.'

'Good,' Eliza said quietly, but with emphasis, and Jack blinked. Did she mean good she didn't have to see *him* till later, or good that the departing matron would show her around?

Strangely, both explanations piqued him and he glanced down at her as they made their way to the front of the hospital. This new matron came up to his shoulder yet her smaller legs didn't seem to have any trouble keeping up with him.

Her hair shone with red glints as they passed under a light and her fringe swung across her face as she turned her head to look up at him. She floated beside him on invisible wings and matched his speed.

'Where's the fire?' She lifted one finely arched brow as she dared him, and he couldn't help smiling at her.

'*Touché*,' he said and slowed. 'I forgot your legs were smaller than mine.'

'Thought you might have,' was all she said, and he realised she jangled his nerves and wasn't overawed by him at all. Well, that was good. Wasn't it?

Jack was pleased to see Mary up ahead.

Matron Mary McGuiness was round-faced and round-bodied, though, of course, most of her abdomen belonged to the baby inside her. Mary *was* the hospital. The staff, and Jack, had a problem imagining anyone else in her position. He hoped Eliza May could do half as good a job in the time she was here.

After the introductions Jack was eager to get away. Most of his eagerness had to do with his waiting patients and a backlog of paper-work, but a percentage had to do with a sudden need to ring his cousin and find out a few more facts about Bellbrook's new Acting Matron. Something about Eliza bothered him.

In fact, several things about her bothered him in a way he hadn't been bothered for years.

He turned to Mary. 'I'll leave Eliza with you, but after showing her around I want you signed off, and with your feet up. Doctor's orders, Mary!' He nodded at Eliza. 'Good luck. You can phone my office if you're worried about anything.'

Eliza smiled blandly. Not if she could help it, Eliza promised herself grimly. Thank goodness he was going. Dr Jack Dancer had everything she wanted to keep away from in a man, let alone one she'd have to totally rely on.

Eliza regretted another bad decision. She may as well rip the heart out of her chest and tear it in two. All he needed was some psychological disaster that kept him from forming a relationship and he'd be irresistible to her twisted mind. After eight weeks with *her* he'd be ready to marry—someone else.

She watched Dr Jack Dancer stride away and Eliza dispassionately imagined she could hear the creak of the fabric stretching across the strong muscles of his long legs and taut backside. Then there were his shoulders.

The man's physical presence was too much. Any woman cradled in Jack Dancer's arms wouldn't be afraid of falling—until he dropped her.

'This will be your office.' Obviously Mary McGuiness hadn't been sidetracked by Jack's physique and Eliza knew *she* was immune. Unobtrusively Eliza dug her nails into her palms to remind herself.

'Do I need an office?' Back on track, Eliza couldn't help returning the other woman's friendly smile because there was something about Mary that warmed the cold parts in Eliza left by too many people over the years. Mary would never let anybody down.

Mary nodded sagely. 'Rosters, hunting up staff if someone is off sick, stock ordering, company reps, interviews with the local news-paper. Heaven forbid—disaster control.'

'Good grief.' Eliza laughed and then stopped, surprised at herself. She hadn't laughed freely for a while. There was such a different feel to this little hospital, a warmth and genuineness that probably radiated from the woman in front of her.

'I'm sure most of those occasions will wait for your return but I can see the need for a private space.' Eliza looked out the door and into the corridor with the clinical areas. 'You say most of my work is hands on?'

'I think you're pleased about that.' Mary smiled again and drew Eliza out of the office. She pointed at doorways as they walked the length of the small building.

'On the semi-acute side, we have two two-bed wards and four single rooms, each with their own bathroom. We were fortunate to build this wing with a bequest from a grateful former client.'

The rooms were light and airy and all the fittings sparkled with good care. Only two of the rooms held patients.

The first room held two men. 'Meet the new matron, gentlemen. This is Eliza May.'

In the bed beside the door, a man in his early thirties had both arms bandaged to the shoulder with just the tips of his fingers poking out the ends.

Mary stopped beside his bed. 'Joe came off worse when he lit a bonfire with too much petrol.' Mary shook her head at his folly.

'Because Joe's hands and arms are involved he needs help to care for himself. He should be in Armidale Hospital but Dr Dancer has a lot of experience with burns and they let Joe come home if he stays here for another few days.'

'Hi, Joe.' Eliza smiled. 'When I was six I fell off my horse and broke both my arms. For six weeks it was hell with no hands. I have a lot of sympathy.'

Joe sighed with relief. 'Reckon you understand, then.'

'Next to Joe is Keith.' Mary smiled at a seventy-ish-looking man with leathery skin and crinkled stockman eyes. 'Keith's supposed to be going home tomorrow. He ruptured his appendix without telling anyone. He wouldn't come in to see the doctor and nearly paid the ultimate price. We've kept him a few extra days to make sure he doesn't work too hard.' Mary narrowed her eyes at the old gentleman. 'I'm not sure he's right yet.'

'Now, Matron.' Keith had a slow drawl and his lilting voice brought back memories to Eliza's mind of her father, as did the seriousness of the old man's expression.

He held out his hand to Eliza. 'Good to meet you, new Matron. I'll shake for Joe and me.'

His work-roughened hand felt cool and welcoming in Eliza's and she began to recall the sweeter side of country towns. These were the facets to country life that the city missed—that she missed—and she had never realised the fact before. Of course she'd never miss anything enough to move from the city permanently and there were aspects of country life that terrified her.

Small towns, gossip, everyone related to everyone else. Eliza had grown up in such a place and shuddered at the memory of when her mother had left them. Her father had closed his door on the wagging tongues, and incidentally Eliza's friends, and she'd never been so lonely. But she didn't want to think about that.

And she didn't want to be drawn into some tiny niche of a town where they would all know her business and invade her personal life.

She'd even told her friend, Julie, at the agency that. 'Bellbrook might be a little too warm and fuzzy for me, the way I'm feeling at the moment,' she'd said, but Julie had seen a benefit that had escaped Eliza.

'There's only one doctor you have to work

with.' Julie had avoided Eliza's eyes when she'd said that, now that Eliza came to think of it.

'Hope you enjoy your stay, Matron.' The old man's kind words penetrated Eliza's reflections and she thanked him and moved on with Mary.

They moved on to the next room and Mary spoke to their only maternity patient. 'This is Janice, and her son Newman.' The baby squawked as if he'd recognised his name and the three women smiled.

'Newman was born two days ago in Armidale by Caesarean, and Janice arrived this morning to convalesce here for the next few days. Meet our new matron, Janice. Eliza May.'

'Congratulations, Janice. He's gorgeous.' Eliza stroked Newman's tiny wrist. She'd read the patient notes later and find out the rest because there'd be a Caesarean story there. She'd always enjoyed her stints in Maternity.

Eliza's not-so-great ex-fiancé, Alex, had been reluctant to even speak of babies and months ago Eliza had decided she'd be better sidetracked by more illness-orientated nursing until her fiancé was ready to discuss children. But she'd missed working in Maternity.

Midwifery was such a fascinating area of nursing. If she wasn't going to get married, maybe she could just enjoy other people's babies.

'He's such a good boy.' Janice's delight in her new son touched Eliza and she saw Mary rest her hand over her stomach. Of course Mary would be anxious for the birth of her own child. Eliza narrowed her eyes as she tried to estimate when Mary's baby was due. Here was an obstetric case right beside her that she needed to keep an eye on.

To Eliza, Mary looked ready to go into labour today!

Maybe that was why Julie had been so keen for Eliza to come here?

They moved on and Eliza glanced in the doors of two empty rooms. 'So do you have many maternity patients?'

Mary nodded. 'We normally have three or four post-delivery patients a month. Each stays for a day or two, sometimes longer.'

'Do you ever have emergency deliveries?'

Mary smiled as if at an amusing memory. 'We can manage if we have to but Jack is so busy with everything else he doesn't feel he can give the care needed and refers any obstetric case on.'

The two women set off again and turned a corner to enter a large dining area with rooms off the other wing. 'Our older residents are on this side of the building and enjoy their meals in the communal dining room when they're well enough.'

They paused at the nurses' station where two identical-looking dark-haired women stood in civilian clothes, waiting to be introduced to Eliza. Another younger woman came up to the desk as introductions were started. They all shook hands and smiled but Eliza had the feeling they were measuring her against Mary. Height wasn't the only thing they were measuring.

Mary continued as her comforting self. 'We have four wonderful enrolled nurses who rotate as the second person on for each shift.' She gestured to a dark-haired young woman. 'This is Vivian, who will be on with you for the rest of the day.'

Eliza smiled at Vivian. A patient call bell rang and Vivian said, 'Nice to meet you.' Then scooted away to answer the summons.

'Rhonda and Donna are our dynamic duo. One of them is your night sister while the other is on days off. They also do the two days on call to cover when you're off. The rest of the week you're the third pair of hands if needed at night.'

Both women nodded and smiled so Eliza gathered she'd passed muster, at least today. 'I'm going home to bed,' Donna said. 'Nice meeting you.'

'I'm off, too. Ditto.' added Rhonda, and they hugged Mary and left.

Mary watched them go and she smiled. 'I'm going to miss this place.' She sighed and then blinked mistily at Eliza and moved on.

Mary cleared her throat. 'Across the hall we have our admissions office and medical records, and in here we have our small emergency room.'

Mary entered the neat mini-theatre and treatment room. 'Of course, very occasionally we have larger emergencies and sometimes use the wards if we need more space.' She gestured to the labelled shelves. 'I'm a big believer in labelling so you shouldn't have any trouble finding things.'

'This is going to be great.' Eliza leant across and rested her arm briefly around Mary's shoulder in a spontaneous gesture of comfort. 'I know I'll love it here, Mary, and you're not to worry. I'll take good care of your hospital until you come back.'

A bell rang overhead and they both glanced up.

'What's the bell for?' Eliza asked, and then frowned as Mary stopped and rested one hand low on her stomach.

'That's the casualty bell. At least I'll get to run you through an outpatient card.'

Eliza inclined her head towards Mary's stomach. 'I'll do this. If you're going into labour I'll write a card for you, too.'

'The tightness will go.' Mary smiled ruefully but didn't deny she had some discomfort as she gingerly led the way round the corner towards the main admissions desk, where a young mother leant on the desk with her frightened daughter by her side.

'Asthma,' the clerk said. 'I'll do the admission without her.' She gladly handed over her charges, along with a dog-eared card.

Eliza glanced at the name. Mia Summers. A good choice by the admissions clerk, Eliza thought as she helped the woman up the hallway until she met Mary with the wheelchair. They wheeled Mia into the assessment room where Eliza sat her on the edge of the bed. Mary hovered at the door, ready to help if Eliza needed her.

At least the woman had been able to stand and hadn't fallen unconscious in the car. It hadn't been that long since Eliza had been present at a young man's tragic death from asthma, and that had been in a big city emergency department with more doctors than they'd needed, but it hadn't been enough. Asthma was a killer if people didn't take the early warning signs seriously enough, and Eliza was on a crusade for education of patients at the moment because of that.

'Hello, Mia. I'm Eliza. Have you got your Ventolin on you?'

Mia opened her mouth to answer but was far too breathless to talk.

'Mummy's puffer is here but she can't seem to breathe it.' The little girl prised the small cylinder from her mother's clenched fist.

Eliza glanced at the label of the puffer and

nodded as she slipped the pulse oximeter on the woman's finger and noted the low oxygen saturation of the woman's blood. She suspected Mia wasn't far from unconsciousness.

'What's your name?' Eliza asked the little girl as she reached up into the cupboard to pull down a Ventolin mask.

'Kristy. I'm eight.'

'I'm Eliza. I think you'll make a great doctor or nurse one day, Kristy, the way you've looked after Mummy. Where's Daddy?'

'Daddy's in the far paddock and Mummy said we had to go now. I left a note.'

'That was clever and Mummy was right.'

While she was talking, Eliza's hands were busy. 'This mask gives Mummy oxygen and makes the stronger asthma drug into a fine mist and that helps Mummy to breathe.'

Eliza broke open the plastic ampoule, squirted the pre-mixed drug into the chamber of the nebulising mask and fitted the now misting mask over Mia's face.

She continued talking to the little girl but really she was talking to the frightened young woman beside her. 'Inside Mummy's lungs, all her little breathing tubes are blocking up with thick slime. This medicine helps the slime get thinner so Mummy can cough it out of the way and breathe better again, and the oxygen makes mummy feel better.'

The little girl nodded and Eliza rested her hand on the woman's shoulder. 'Just close your eyes, Mia, and let the medication do the job.' Eliza fitted the blood-pressure cuff around the woman's arm and began to pump it up. 'Do you have an asthma plan sheet and a spacer?'

Mia shook her head tiredly and Eliza nodded. 'We'll talk about it later because I think it would help a lot in your case.'

Eliza glanced at Mary. 'She needs IV access, cortisone and probably IV salbutamol. Would you like to ring Dr Dancer to come around? I'll pop a cannula in to save time.'

Mary nodded and reached for the phone on

the wall while Eliza swiftly prepared her equipment. 'I'm going to put a little needle in Mummy's arm. It looks like it would hurt but it's really not much more than a mosquito bite. Mummy needs some other medicine that works really quickly if we put it in through the needle. Do you want to look away when I do it?'

Kristy shook her head. 'I'll hold Mummy's other hand.'

'You have a wonderful daughter, Mia.'

Mia nodded as she started to cough. Already her oxygen saturation had improved. Eliza glanced at Kristy to see if she was upset by her mother coughing.

'So the slime in Mummy's lungs is getting thinner, isn't it Eliza?'

'Yep.' Eliza slid the cannula into Mia's arm and taped it securely. Then she began to assemble the flask and line and draw up the drugs in preparation. 'Next time Mummy's fingers go this blue or she can't talk, she'd better come in the ambulance because they can give her this medicine in the mask and put the needle in on the way to the doctor. Do you know how to ring an ambulance, Kristy?'

Kristy nodded. 'I ring 000, or 911 in America or 999 in England.'

'Wow. Even I didn't know that.' Eliza felt like hugging the little girl. 'Tell them Mummy can't breathe and then answer all the questions.'

When Jack arrived he could see that Eliza had everything under control. Mia could manage a few words, and after he approved the intravenous drugs Eliza had ready, Mia was stable enough to go by ambulance to Armidale, where she'd have to stay overnight, at the very least, for intensive observation.

'Rhonda's coming in as escort in the ambulance with you, Mia.' Jack squeezed the young woman's shoulder. 'If all goes well, I'll see if they'll transfer you back to us here at Bellbrook tomorrow or the day after.'

Mia's husband arrived. Jack reaffirmed Mia would be better in Armidale, at least overnight, and after goodbyes Mr Summers took their daughter home.

Jack watched Eliza clear the benches and restock the room in record time. He shook his head. Good was an understatement. He wasn't sure he was used to someone telling him what he needed to give a patient, but he'd have to get over it. Eliza had certainly been instrumental in saving Mia's condition from becoming perilous, and that was the important thing.

He cleared his throat and wondered why the words stuck a little. 'You did well, Eliza. Mia hasn't had an attack that severe before.'

Eliza stopped what she was doing and met his eyes. He watched her smile spread to her eyes at his compliment and he could feel himself responding. She was like a sunrise. Boom—explosion of light as she smiled. She blew him away again just like she had when he'd first met her.

'Thank you,' she said quietly. 'So this is what a sleepy country town is like.'

The moment extended and his smile broadened. She was gorgeous in an understated way and his diaphragm imploded again. Unconsciously he took a step forward towards her, as if it was the most natural thing in the world to want to be closer to her.

Then she changed and the corners of her mouth drooped. The expression in her beautiful eyes grew distant and she broke eye contact as she looked away. The angry fairy wasn't quite back but there were glimpses.

Eliza spoke to the package she lifted into the cupboard. 'Mia said she doesn't have an asthma plan or a spacer. Are the plans not something you do here?'

'Not really.' Jack didn't concentrate too much on what she was saying because he was wondering why she'd created such reserve and backed away from being friendly. He refocussed on her question. 'If someone becomes a moderate asthmatic, I usually send them to a specialist in Armidale or even the re-

spiratory clinic in Newcastle, and the special-
ists do all that.'

She twisted her neck and looked at him from
under her brows. 'I'll have some forms sent
from the Asthma Foundation. They'll send us
an info pack and a pad of plans that you could
look at. I've helped generate plans before and
believe they give the patient back control of
their asthma. Spacers make it easier for the
patient to take their Ventolin, especially
during an attack.'

Her tone was icy and he couldn't help the
drop in warmth in his own voice. It was almost
as if she'd engineered the whole estrangement
of their brief rapport. Something else was
going on here, something ill-defined, and he
didn't like it, but he had to get back to his
surgery. If she didn't want him here, he could
take a hint!

'Thank you, Matron May. I've actually seen
such plans and I know what a spacer is,' Jack
said dryly. 'I'll certainly consider your sugges-

tion.' He glanced at the door where Mary was an interested bystander. 'I thought you were going home, Mary?'

Mary raised placatory hands and bit back a smile. 'I just need to finish the round I've started with Eliza. I'll be gone soon.'

'Well, I *am* gone,' Jack muttered. 'Matrons,' he said mockingly, and inclined his head at Eliza. Then he took himself back to his surgery.

Eliza watched him go. What on earth had got into her? Lecturing Jack! It wasn't part of her job and she didn't need to alienate her boss for the next eight weeks.

And why was she thinking of him as Jack and not Dr Dancer?

The problem was, the guy was too tall, too handsome and too sure of himself, and he made her feel all weak and feminine and things she'd promised she wasn't going to feel again. What really worried her was whether coming here had been another bad decision. She'd made a few of those in her life.

'I'm afraid I've put his back up,' Eliza said.

'You don't look too upset about it. It won't kill him to have someone not in awe of him.' Mary changed the subject. 'You seemed to find everything you needed for Mia easily.'

Eliza glanced around at the now tidy room. Back to reality and escape from the distraction of Dr Jack Dancer. 'You've stored everything in the most obvious place, Mary, and the labelling is fantastic. This is such a bonus. As an agency nurse, finding the equipment is the hardest part.'

'I'll bet.' Mary tilted her head. 'So how did you get into agency work? I bet a few hospitals would love to hire you full-time with your qualifications.'

Eliza met Mary's eyes. 'It's a new direction for me. I like being unattached. It gives me the choice to move when I want to.'

'Fair enough,' Mary said. 'We'll move on ourselves before Jack discovers me here on his next round.' She smiled and swayed out of the room to waddle further down the hallway.

'Where was I? Basically, you do five days a week, eight hours normal and four hours overtime, then you're on call at night except for weekends. Think you can handle that?'

'Fine by me.' Eliza shook her head at Mary. 'How on earth did you have time to fall pregnant?'

Mary twinkled back. 'My husband is the local fire captain, amongst other things, so we know there's twenty-four hours in a day. We both enjoy being busy. He's away at a conference at the moment.'

Mary shrugged. 'When Mick's home he's home and when he's not I spend a lot of time here. We both like it that way. He used to be in the navy.' She answered the question Eliza didn't ask. 'Mick will be home in a few days and stick around more when my baby is due.'

'And if baby comes early?' They both glanced down at Mary's stomach.

'He'll have to fly home quick smart!'

Eliza shook her head at Mary's calmness. 'Mary, I think you're Wonder Woman.'

Mary shrugged. 'I'll be Bored Woman for the next few weeks. I wondered if you'd like to drop around in a day or so. I'm sure you'll have questions and I'll be dying to know how you settle in.'

And that's how country towns worked. Eliza knew that from past experience. It wasn't what she'd planned when she'd hoped to keep a city-dweller's distance from the townsfolk. She'd seen the effect of gossip and everyone knowing her business, but she couldn't offend Mary. Bellbrook's matron was too genuine.

Trouble was the next thing would be an in-depth conversation with the publican's wife when she went back to the hotel tonight. Then there'd be the corner shop purchases tomorrow and the visit to the post office, by which time everyone in the valley would be aware of her arrival, the car she drove and enough physical features to be picked out at a hundred paces.

She'd better not do anything noteworthy or Jack Dancer, who seemed to be related to everyone, would be the first to hear about it.

CHAPTER TWO

BY LUNCHTIME Mary had departed to rest as ordered by her doctor.

Eliza glanced around at the eight elderly patients seated at the dining table to eat their lunch. She'd handed out the medications and done a ward tidy with Vivian.

If Eliza looked on the workload as just a normal ward with diverse patients, and not a whole hospital, there was nothing she hadn't done before.

By six-thirty that evening she'd found most things she could possibly need, had had in-depth conversations with all the inpatients, as well as read their medical records and helped with the evening meal.

She'd glanced through the rosters to see how they worked and spent ten minutes on the phone to Julie, her friend at the nursing agency, to say she was settling in.

Now all she had to do was a ward round with the distracting Dr Dancer and she'd be finished for the day.

Eliza glanced at the clock again and drummed her fingers on the nurses' station desk.

He was late.

She was getting more unsettled by the minute with a waiting-for-the-dentist kind of tension and Eliza wished he'd just arrive. Surely Dancer wasn't so spectacular he'd turned her into a bundle of nerves?

Apparently he was. When Jack breezed in he brought more devastation to her peace of mind than she needed. So much for saying her imagination had been over-active. His wavy black hair was tousled as if he'd been dragging distracted hands through it all day, and he'd even jammed a couple of curls behind his ears.

That was when she noticed he had a tiny diamond in his right ear lobe. How on earth had she missed that this morning?

'Ready for the round?' He seemed very businesslike and Eliza allowed some of the tightness to ease from her shoulders. Businesslike sounded good. He'd want to get home, too. The brusquer the better, Eliza thought gratefully.

'Let's go.' She picked up a notebook in case she needed to take notes.

He glanced across at her briefly, and she saw he had dark chocolate eyes, not black, as she'd previously thought, a strange thing to notice when she was supposed to be immune.

'So how was your day?' Jack was brief and Eliza even briefer.

'Fine.' She picked up the pace to get the next few minutes over as quickly as possible. Noticing too many things about this man, Eliza, she thought grimly.

'Are we racing again?' Laughter in his voice and Eliza felt her face stiffen. Please, don't let him be nice to me or flirt with me or in any way endear himself to me, she prayed. There was something about him that pierced her skin like a poison dart and was just as irritating. She was not playing man games any more.

'I just know you'll be emotionally scarred and unable to have a worthwhile relationship,' she muttered.

Jack stopped walking and Eliza carried on a few more steps before she realised she'd said what was on her mind out loud! She closed her eyes and then opened them again. Oh, boy!

He tilted his head. 'I'm sorry? What did you say?'

She glanced down and then lifted her chin resolutely. 'Sorry. Ignore that.'

He looked stunned.

She shrugged. 'Look, I may seem mad, but I've had the worst run of luck with men and I'm still spinning from the last one. I seem to have a penchant for poor sods who have been a victim of some unscrupulous woman. They find me, I heal their poor broken hearts, and then they happily marry someone else. I usually get invited to the wedding. For some bizarre reason, I don't want to play that game any more.'

She was sure his eyes were glazing over but it was imperative she make this clear. 'This may seem more than you need to know, but I am trying to explain my stupid comment.'

He moved his lips a little but didn't actually say a word. Eliza sighed. 'Forget I spoke and we'll do the ward round.'

Jack felt as if someone had just popped a paper bag in his unsuspecting face. He'd known there was something odd about her. The chameleon fairy was mad and Mary was gone. What the heck were they going to do? He'd had a hell of a day already.

After the dash out for Mia's asthma attack, he'd returned to his office and realised today was the anniversary of the worst day of his life. He hadn't been able to believe it had slipped his mind for a few hours.

After he'd fought his way out of that depression, a desperate young couple, distant relatives on his mother's side, had miscarried their second IVF baby. Then one of his uncles had come in for results on a mole he'd excised last week, and the specimen had proved to be a particularly vicious melanoma.

Now this!

The new fairy matron was a man-hating elf with issues.

He heard her voice from a long way off. 'It's OK,' she said. 'Forget it.'

He blinked, the hallway came into focus again, and he shelved her replacement problems for a minute. Deep breath, Jack, he suggested to himself.

She was still talking as if nothing had happened. 'You should have a look at Keith's wound. I know he's supposed to go home tomorrow but I believe he's brewing an infection.'

Jack blinked. He'd just play along with her

until after the round. 'Fine. I'll look at that. How's Keith's temperature?'

'Creeping up, and it spiked to thirty-nine this afternoon before it went down again.'

Jack glanced at the chart the madwoman handed him from the end of Keith's bed and he saw that she was right. Blast. They'd have to start intravenous antibiotics again because Keith had little reserve to fight infection after his brush with peritonitis.

She'd pulled the curtains and had Keith supine in the bed with his shirt up before Jack could ask, and when she removed the dressing, tell-tale red streaks were inching away from Keith's wound.

He glanced at Keith's face and realised his patient did look more unwell than this morning. 'Sorry, Keith. No home until we sort this out.'

Keith sighed with resignation. 'Matron warned me it could be that way.'

Eliza spoke from beside his shoulder. 'Do you want me to put an intravenous cannula in?' Jack saw that she had the IV trolley

waiting and she'd probably decided which antibiotics Keith should be on, too. Just who was
the doctor here? He couldn't help the bite in
his voice. 'Have you drawn it up as well?'

He should have known she'd be immune.

'Almost,' she said. Was there a hint of
laughter in her voice?

Jack scowled. She went on, 'What would
you like him started on?'

She had two choices there for him and they
would have been first and second if he'd
chosen them himself. What was wrong with
him? He wanted her efficient. 'We'll go with
the Ceftriaxone, but see if you can get a wound
swab before the first dose.'

She didn't look at him and he couldn't tell
if she was smiling. 'Did that earlier when I
took today's dressing off,' she said, as she
prepared the antibiotic before laying it down
and assembling the cannulation equipment.

'Shall I pop the cannula in?' Eliza glanced
at him.

Jack almost said, I'll do that thank you, but he changed his mind. 'Let's see how good you are,' he said out loud. Nothing like a bit of pressure to put someone off. He knew from bitter experience that Keith's veins were nowhere near the young bulging ones that Mia had. Matron May was too darned cocky.

'Just a sting for a second, Keith,' Eliza soothed as she slid the needle into an almost invisible vein with disgusting ease. She seemed to have three hands as she juggled cannulas, bungs and even took blood. 'Did you want blood cultures?' She taped the line securely and stood back. They both glanced at the antibiotic waiting to be injected.

'Can I do this?' He sounded petty and she made a strange sound that he hoped wasn't her laughing at him. He normally wasn't like this and he needed to get a grip. He looked at her to apologise but realised she *was* amused. Amused!

Today had been anything but amusing. He

didn't say a word, just gave the antibiotic, wrote up the orders and patted Keith's hand carefully. 'Sorry, mate. You'll probably be in for another couple of days yet.'

Keith nodded. When they pulled the curtain back Jack was surprised to see that Joe was asleep. He frowned and raised his eyebrows at Eliza and she drew him from the room.

'I found out today he hasn't been taking any pain relief. He didn't want Keith to think he was a baby,' she said quietly, and shrugged. 'I spoke to Joe when Keith was out of the room and we've come to an agreement. Since the first lot of medication he's been asleep and Keith tells me Joe's hardly slept.'

Jack frowned and then nodded. 'OK. Let's get on, then.'

They completed the round and had a quick look at Janice and her baby in less than ten minutes. There was very little conversation between them.

As he was leaving, Jack looked back and paused. He had been abrupt. 'Matron?'

Eliza glanced up from the notes she was making. 'Yes, Doctor?'

'Well done with the cannula, and Joe as well. If I seem brusque, I've had a wild day.'

'No problem.' The woman seemed to be staring at some point over his left shoulder and disinclined to talk, so Jack forced himself to leave. It was surprisingly hard to take that first step away. He was more confused about her than ever and he didn't like it. Until today his world had been pleasantly uncomplicated.

He'd put the horror of three years ago behind him and he'd immersed himself in work. He'd assumed he'd get married again someday but hadn't dated a woman since Lydia had died.

And he wasn't thinking of dating this one— but she certainly unsettled him.

* * *

Eliza headed back to the hotel. Except for a young blonde woman reading in the corner, the bar was quiet as she walked past the door.

'So you're the new matron,' the blonde drawled, and Eliza's step slowed to a stop.

'Hello.'

'Staying here will get a little noisy on a Friday night.'

'I'll be fine.' Eliza smiled and crossed the room to hold out her hand. 'I'm Eliza May.'

'Carla.' There was something elusively appealing about this too-thin girl-woman and then there was the ice that frosted the outside of her glass in the cloying heat.

Eliza licked dry lips and put her handbag down on the stool beside the girl. 'It's hot this evening.'

'Always is this time of the year.' Carla stood up, walked behind the bar and filled a glass with ice. Then she opened an under-bar fridge and removed a beaded bottle of lemon squash and unscrewed the lid. 'I should ask you first.' She grinned. 'But you'd like a squash, wouldn't you.'

Eliza grinned back at her. 'Dying for one! Thank you. Do you work here?'

'No. Rob's gone to the loo. I'm just minding the bar for a minute.'

Carla glanced out the door and back. 'I'm off for a swim in the river when I finish my drink. If you want, I'll show you a spot you can swim in when the days are like this.'

'Local knowledge.' Eliza smiled as she put two dollars down on the bar for her drink. She remembered local knowledge as a child, it had usually got her into trouble.

'Something like that.' There was a hint of fun which dared Eliza to take her up on the offer. After the unease she'd felt round Jack Dancer, it would be nice to loosen up and get cool.

Eliza downed her squash. 'I'll slip up and grab a towel.'

The swimming hole was through two fences at the back of the pub but worth the climb down a steep bank to get to. It was under a cliff face and two large weeping willows shaded the pool. There was an aging PRIVATE PROPERTY sign, adorned with a few grass necklaces from previous floods, prominently displayed near the edge.

Carla ignored it. The water looked too good to forgo.

Eliza yanked down the sides of her bathers—they seemed to like crawling too high on her leg and up her bottom. She stood hesitantly at the edge. She hated wearing swimming costumes because they made her feel so self-conscious. Carla was already in and the water looked wonderful.

The first step wasn't too bad and the temperature of the water grew colder the further out through the reeds Eliza walked.

'It's freezing,' Eliza gasped. The shock on her face when she finally forced her whole body under the water made Carla laugh when Eliza surfaced beside her.

'Yep.' Carla swam languidly across the pool

and Eliza watched her for a moment before she turned on her back and floated with her arms out. The icy water was gorgeous against her heated skin. This had been an excellent idea.

'Get out of there!'

Eliza recognised that voice and the enjoyment drained out of the moment as if he'd pulled the plug.

'You know better, Carla.' Jack Dancer was cross, there was no doubt about that, Eliza thought, and her heart pumped as if she were a ten-year-old again caught crossing a forbidden field.

'You're such a sourpuss, Dr Jack,' Carla said as she drifted languidly to the shallow water.

'It would serve you right if you got bitten by a bullrout. Smithy was stung here yesterday and you wouldn't be so relaxed if you'd seen his face as I filled him up with morphine. But you shouldn't have put Eliza at risk—she'd from the city and probably doesn't know what a bullrout is.'

'I know what a bullrout is,' Eliza said quietly. The camouflaged fresh-water fish could look like a rock and wore three venom pouches on its spines. Its sting was excruciating. She glanced warily at the reeds as she followed Carla out of the water. The spot was lovely but not worth those kinds of stings. Eliza wrapped her arms around her blatant nipples. Well, the water had been cold, for crikey's sake. Now she had to get out of here, wet, bathers glued to her too-generous curves, and all under the gaze of that man. The day just kept getting better and better. Eliza compressed her lips.

Finally both women stood at the edge of the innocent-looking water wrapped in towels. They both glared across at the man on the opposite bank.

Carla tossed her hair and turned her back on Jack. 'You can go home happy, now, you grump. You've spoiled our swim so you can relax.'

Jack didn't say anything or seem perturbed

by Carla's rudeness, and Eliza stood indecisively. She resisted her own impulse to emulate Carla but had the maturity to realise it was a response to being caught in the wrong. Even worse, she hated being caught in her bathers. It was too late to worry now. She half waved to a still waiting Jack and followed Carla up the bank.

When they got to the top, Eliza was almost as hot as when she'd started and not all of it from the sun. She should have gone with her instincts and avoided the local knowledge.

'Sorry about that.' Carla held up her hands in an I-didn't-mean-for-that-to-happen gesture. 'No one's been stung there for two years. I didn't know about Smithy. It's such a top spot if Dr Jack doesn't catch you.'

'So Jack polices the waterholes as well as does the doctoring?' Eliza could see the amusing part of being caught by Jack—just.

'He owns the land on both sides of the river,' Carla said as she headed back to the pub. She glanced over her shoulder to Eliza. 'But nobody owns the river.'

The next day every person Eliza met in the hospital mentioned her being caught by Jack down at the rout waterhole. She knew there was a reason she'd avoided returning to the country.

Apparently Carla's friend Rob from the pub thought it a hilarious story and had mentioned it to everyone who'd come into the hotel. They'd passed it on to anyone they'd seen in the next twelve hours and by the time Eliza came to work the story had been embellished to include her and Carla topless with a few men from the pub watching.

'Spare me.' Eliza closed her eyes and shook her head. Janice tried to stifle her giggle so as not to wake her baby but she was having a hard time of it.

'The topless bit was from old Pat, and nobody really believes him, but it seems you've made a name for yourself as a good sport already.'

'Well, I hope nobody believes "Old Pat". If I meet that delightful old gentleman for a tetanus shot, he's in for a larger-than-normal-gauge needle.'

Janice dissolved into giggles again and Eliza had to smile at her, but the smile disappeared when Jack Dancer walked into the room.

The memory of him watching her as she'd left the water yesterday warmed her cheeks and she fought the sudden urge to fold her arms again. She was too darned aware of this guy and survival meant he wasn't to know.

'All well in here, ladies?' Jack's face was expressionless but Eliza suspected a twinkle behind those pseudo black eyes of his. The swine.

'Eliza was just saying how hot it was yesterday,' Janice said cheekily, but Jack wasn't playing.

'Yes, it was. How's Newman this morning, Janice?'

Eliza tried to let her relieved breath out un-obtrusively as Jack concentrated on his patient.

Janice went on. 'Fine. We're both fine. My mum arrives from Melbourne today so he's going to meet his nana when she comes in to visit.'

'Say hello to your mum for me if I don't see her.' He stepped back from the cot. 'I've a lot on this morning so I'll leave you in Matron's capable hands.'

Eliza followed him out of the room. She hoped he didn't think she'd been discussing yesterday. 'I didn't tell her. Apparently it's all over town that you chased us out of the river.'

Jack glanced up from the notes he car-ried. 'Bellbrook is a small town. People find out and embellish all the time.' He looked at her fully and she saw the wicked twinkle in his eyes. 'I particularly enjoyed the naked version, with me throwing you a towel.'

Eliza rested her hand over her mouth as she felt the heat rise again in her face. Then she surprised herself with a tiny gurgle of laughter as the funny side of the situation tickled her again.

Just when he thought he had her on the back foot she surprised him again. Jack had spent most of the night trying to rid himself of delightful memories of Eliza, tiny but perfectly packaged, as she'd stepped from the water.

Intriguingly, her breasts had been stunningly full and globular beneath the wet one-piece costume as she'd bent to pick up the towel. Even now that day-old snapshot in his mind made his mouth dry.

Her breasts hadn't jumped out at him yesterday morning, he mused, and then his own sense of humour caught up with him. Impossible fantasy. He pulled himself back under control and tried to quieten the sudden increase in his heart rate. Now she was giving him palpitations. What on earth was the matter with him?

'Most people from the city would have a problem with being the object of small-town gossip,' Jack said without looking at her.

'I'm not "most people",' she replied calmly, and began to talk about Keith, but he didn't believe her. Her cheeks were just a little too rosy.

By the end of the round Jack was again impressed with Eliza's ability to manage situations. She'd steered him back onto the job, calmed Keith despite the older man being bitterly disappointed he'd be laid up for probably another week, managed the most painless removal of Joe's dressing they'd had yet, and was obviously a favourite with the seniors on the wing.

'You're doing a great job, Matron. It feels like you've been here for much longer than a day and a half.'

'It feels like that to me, too,' Eliza said dryly.

Jack wondered at her parting comment as he walked around the side of the hospital to his surgery. The woman intrigued him far too much and he didn't think she was immune to him either.

CHAPTER THREE

THE next day Jack had meetings in Armidale after the morning round and wouldn't be back until late. The day was uneventful for Eliza and she felt unsettled after the shift had finished. So much so that she decided to go for a drive.

Eliza glanced down at the directions Mary had pressed on her and judged she was nearly there. The powerful vehicle purred along the dirt road and hugged the uneven surface with ease.

The Mustang was almost forty years old and a classic. With the top down she could blow all her worries into tomorrow. She loved this car. It had been her father's pride and joy and she'd taken it to Sydney with her when she'd moved there.

She refused to think about Jack Dancer because she'd spent the last hour beating herself up over wondering if he'd make it for the last round after all. He had.

She wasn't sure if visiting Mary was the most sensible thing to do if she wanted to stay immune to involvement in this town. Though Mary seemed to be one of the few people who wasn't related to Dr Jack. And Eliza had promised an update of her first few days.

The Mustang pulled up outside the McGuiness property and Mary was at the door before Eliza could walk halfway to the front steps.

Mary's smile was almost as big as her pregnant tummy. 'How are you? Is everything going smoothly? How are you coping with Jack?'

Eliza stood there, felt her face freeze and wished she hadn't come. And the worst thing was, Mary picked it up immediately. Her grin faltered. 'I'm sorry, Eliza. Come in and I promise I won't ask about anything else. I was just so excited about getting a visitor.'

Eliza had to smile. 'So you've had thirty-six hours of maternity leave and already you're feeling socially isolated?'

'Pathetic isn't it?' Mary led them into a sunny room that faced west. There was a long purple mountain range in the distance and Mary's house perched on a rise overlooking a huge dam. Most of the sprawling garden comprised hardy native plants and birds darted in and out of the low foliage.

'It's beautiful here.'

'Yes, it is. But now that I'm having a baby I wish we were closer to town.' Mary showed her to a rose-patterned lounge suite and they both sat down.

Eliza sank into the cushions and sighed as she felt the tension from Jack's latest hospital round ease away into the soft upholstery.

She looked across at Mary perched on the

adjacent chair, a little forlorn-looking. 'Can't your husband come home earlier?'

'He could but then he'd have to travel sooner after our baby is born and we want as much time as a family in the early months as we can.'

'That makes sense. I think. So what are you going to do with your bundle of joy when you go back to work?'

Mary smiled. 'That's what's so special about Bellbrook. I'll take my baby with me. The hospital isn't really much more than a large family home and there're always plenty of hands ready to help if I need.' They both laughed and Eliza began to enjoy herself.

'Come for a walk in the garden,' Mary said, 'before the sun goes down. It's a lovely time of the evening.'

Eliza followed Mary out onto the patio and the scent of bush roses drifted up from the path. She'd often enjoyed long walks with her father around the farm.

Three black cockatoos took off from a gum

tree and their raucous cries almost drowned Mary out as they flew away.

Eliza said 'Three days' rain' at the same time as Mary, and then laughed. 'So you're superstitious, too?'

'Aren't we all?' Mary sidestepped a ladder against the wall and they both had the giggles again.

'I always thought country people seem more prone to superstitions than city folk,' Eliza mused.

Mary looked up with interest. 'So are you really a country girl at heart?'

'My dad loved the country. I didn't mind it.'

'And your mother?'

Eliza shrugged. 'She left because of it. And the gossip, my dad said.'

Mary nodded. 'This place thrives on gossip.'

'Then I supposed you heard about Carla and I being hunted out of the river by Jack?'

Mary's eyes twinkled. 'I was hoping you'd mention that!'

Eliza held up both hands and shook her head. 'I'm innocent, I swear.' And then she started to laugh at the memory of herself cowering in the river. 'People even said I was naked and Jack threw me a towel.'

'You mean that didn't happen?' Mary looked crestfallen but couldn't hold the expression long enough for Eliza to believe she was serious. They both laughed again.

'Gossip comes because a lot of people are related in small towns—even if only by marriage.'

Eliza remembered the speed of the informants. 'So how many people are related to Jack Dancer?'

The question seemed to come from nowhere but it was too late for Eliza to call it back. She hoped Mary wouldn't assume she was becoming interested in Jack because she had the feeling matchmaking was a latent facet of Mary's personality.

Mary shrugged. 'Most of us are related in some way.'

Eliza nodded and rolled her eyes. 'So I've noticed. Does that mean you're a part of Jack's enormous family circle?'

Mary sighed. 'I'm not really. Originally, I was from Sydney.' There was sadness in Mary's voice and Eliza refrained from asking the obvious question.

'Jack's great-grandparents started it all when they had ten kids and most of them settled here. Jack has more cousins than a dog has fleas.'

Eliza had a sudden vision of a giant Jack with cousins crawling all over him, and she smiled. 'So why isn't Jack married with ten kids?'

'That's the crux of his problem. He was. Jack married my sister. She died three years ago.' Mary trailed off for a moment then shook her head to jolt herself out of the melancholy.

'Lydia didn't like the life in Bellbrook and went back to Sydney. She and their unborn baby boy were killed in a car crash a month later.'

Eliza felt the breath catch in her throat. Poor Jack. 'That's sad for everyone. It must have been hard for both you and Jack.'

Mary gazed in the direction of the distant hills. 'Jack looked after me. My husband, Mick, hadn't really liked Lydia, and when she left Jack, Mick washed his hands of her. Jack always has had that caring quality that forgives and shoulders responsibility, and I guess that was some of what my sister saw when she married him.'

Mary went on slowly. 'Lydia was different from me. Beautiful, spoiled by my parents, a talented arts major. And she hated Bellbrook. Then she hated being pregnant. In the end, she hated Jack.'

Mary looked down at her bulging belly and smiled.

'I love pregnancy and I love Bellbrook and…' Mary smiled softly, '…like a brother, I love Jack.'

Mary's face softened even further with a

whimsical smile. 'Thanks to Jack, I met my husband, Mick. He was best man at Jack and Lydia's wedding. We fell in love and married in about three days. I've felt at home here ever since. Life is funny with what it deals out.'

So there were good love stories out there, Eliza sighed. Mary looked so content with her life and her love. Lucky Mary. Eliza herself *definitely* wasn't interested in taking any more chances with love.

But she was curious about the dashing Dr Dancer's wife. How could any woman hate Jack? 'What did your sister do here?'

'Nothing. We tried to get her involved in community activities, tennis, I suggested she run an art class for the town but she wasn't interested. She was bored silly and became very bitter at wasting her life, as she called it. Before Lydia died, I'd even decided it hadn't been a bad thing she'd left, because she had made Jack so unhappy. I think Jack was leaning that way too, until the crash.'

Mary shook her head sadly. 'I went to pieces. Jack and I both felt so guilty because maybe we should have supported Lydia more. Jack was devastated about the loss of his son as well. He blamed himself and Lydia's pregnancy for making her temperamental, as if if he'd paid more attention to her she wouldn't have left and his son would be alive today.' Mary sighed.

'Jack studied up on maternal trauma and resuscitation of pregnant women for months afterwards, wondering if the hospital she had been taken to should have done anything different when Lydia was brought in barely alive.' She looked at Eliza.

'I think it's still all locked away inside him behind his carefree smile. I guess that's why he's not in a hurry to marry again.'

Mary patted her stomach. 'He said he'd leave all the hassle of kids to me and be a doting uncle. I think it's a shame—and watch out. Everyone in town agrees.'

Eliza felt a flicker of panic at Mary's hint. 'Don't look at me. I'm off men.'

Mary looked across at Eliza. 'That doesn't matter. You'd better be prepared for some matchmaking uncles and aunts because they'd all like nothing better than to see Jack settled with a family here.'

As they turned towards the back door the sound of a car pulling up outside coincided with the ringing of the telephone. Mary looked torn and Eliza shrugged. 'I'll get the door, you take the phone.'

Eliza wished she'd taken the phone because she was still affected by the conversation with Mary and the visitor was Jack.

'What are you doing here?' They both spoke and Eliza shook her head. Her whole life was a cliché.

'Snap!' She shrugged and stood back so he could enter. 'Mary's on the phone. She shouldn't be long.'

Jack's mouth twitched wryly. 'Unless it's

her husband, in which case the record is three hours and ten minutes.'

Eliza whistled. She did not need three hours and ten minutes of Jack. Just looking at him jangled her nerves, and with all the new insight from Mary she didn't know how to cope with him. 'Tell Mary I'll come back another day. I'm tired anyway.'

He looked out the window to Eliza's car and grimaced. 'Is that your Mustang?'

Eliza's gaze shifted to the now dusty red duco of her car. 'That's my baby.'

'How much fossil fuel does it use?'

She glanced in the direction Mary had disappeared but relief wasn't in sight. There were undercurrents. 'That depends how I drive it, Doctor.'

When she looked back at him his face was hard. 'And how do you drive it?'

She shook her head. 'What possible interest could that be to you?'

She thought he wasn't going to answer that

one but he did and she almost wished he hadn't. 'I don't like waste of life and a car like that just isn't as safe as the modern vehicles of today.'

'I'll be at work tomorrow. Don't worry.' She put her hand in her pocket and pulled out her car keys. 'Please, tell Mary I'll catch up with her later. Goodnight.'

Eliza didn't gun the engine but she would have liked to. Jack Dancer, emotionally scarred human being—she'd known it. Someone up there was plotting against her, although she had to admit Jack had had a tough couple of years.

Jack watched the dust ball disappear down the road just as he'd watched another car when his wife had left him to settle back into the city. He turned at the sound of Mary's footsteps and she crossed to his side and kissed his cheek.

'I think she'll be good for the town,' Jack said.

'She could be good for you,' Mary said slyly. His emotions were still too mixed when it came to Eliza May. 'I didn't come here to talk about Eliza.'

'Why not? We talked about you.'

Jack lifted his brows but refused to bite. Mary lowered herself into a chair. 'So why did you come?'

'To see you.'

'And why has Eliza gone?'

'She said she'll come back another time.' He turned to face Mary. 'Workwise, she's good. If she stays, we'll manage fine until you feel like coming back.'

'You *are* being nice to her, aren't you, Jack?'

Jack shrugged. 'Not too nice. I think she has a lot of emotional baggage.'

'And you don't?'

His face hardened again and he changed the subject. 'I can't stay. Just wanted to see how you like being on maternity leave.'

'Putting my feet up is bliss but I think I'm going to go stark raving mad without something to occupy my brain. Stay and have tea with me. I was planning on persuading Eliza to stay but you chased her away.'

'I didn't chase her away,' he said, but he wondered if that was wholly true. He had to admit that so far the new matron had not brought out the best in him, and maybe that was because she scared him a little. Not physically—tiny bundle that she was—but at some deep instinctual level that he didn't want to think about. Maybe he owed Mary his company.

'Fine. Tea would be great. I've had a less-than-perfect day and not having to cook the evening meal will brighten the end of it.'

'I've told you before. You should get a housekeeper and she could prepare your meal before she leaves for the day.'

'I know, but I like my privacy, and you know what this town is like.' He followed Mary into the kitchen and tried to make his next comment seem inconsequential. 'I rang Julie again today and apparently she and Eliza are friends. She said she's very reliable.'

Mary tilted her head at him and he knew what she was thinking before she said it. 'Now, why would you do that? I thought you said you were satisfied with her work.' Trust Mary to question his motives.

'I decided to listen to my instincts.'

'Well, my instincts say that there is a wonderful woman inside Eliza May, and already I count her as a friend.' She looked at him as if daring him to comment, but he wasn't that silly. When he kept his peace, she nodded. 'Let's eat. I was thinking we might dine outside because it's such a lovely evening.'

'Good morning, Matron.'

Jack was all *bonhomie* this morning, Eliza thought sourly. Her back and legs ached from a third night on the lumpiest mattress in the southern hemisphere but that wasn't the real reason she hadn't slept. Her eyes felt scratchy from lack of sleep.

'Morning.' She turned from his scrutiny but he was observant.

'You don't look like you slept well.'

'I'll make the hotel a present of a new mattress.'

'Like that, was it?' He seemed determined to be nice and Eliza could feel herself softening more towards him—no doubt because she'd tossed and turned thinking over Mary's revelations last night.

'Hmm,' she said, and changed the subject, opting for safety. 'Keith looks a little better this morning so I gather the antibiotics are kicking in.'

They walked down the hallway together and now she was aware of his height beside her and when he smiled and even the sound of his feet quietly pacing beside her. She couldn't switch off her awareness of him. This was not good. She began to edge away from him.

He seemed oblivious. 'I'm pleased. And did Joe sleep better than you did?'

What was with the personal comments this morning? She remembered his tone last night when he'd been anything but friendly—of course, she'd left him with Mary so he'd probably had instructions to lift his game. Please, don't encourage him, she prayed to the absent Mary.

Eliza needed to create some space, quickly, until she could build her defences again. 'Did Mary tell you to be nice to me this morning?'

He actually blushed. Eliza felt mean, but he did withdraw. Ironically, a part of her regretted his distance now but the sensible Eliza sighed with relief.

They crossed to the little maternity room. Janice had Newman floating in the baby bath with the back of his neck draped across his mother's wrist. Mother and baby both looked relaxed.

'You're an old hand at this, Janice,' Jack said. He stared down at Newman, who floated with his eyes open, staring up at his mother.

He was a cute little fellow, Jack thought, and this time the pain of his own loss didn't follow as strongly as it usually did.

'He loves his bath.' Janice smiled as she glanced up.

'How're your tummy stitches? Not too painful?' Janice seemed to be standing up straight enough, Jack thought.

'No. I'm fine. Eliza gave me some tablets earlier so I could enjoy giving Newman his bath, and we're both going to have a sleep after this.'

'How's he feeding?' On cue, Newman burped loudly and they all laughed.

'Piggy,' his mother said, and she grinned up at Jack. 'He feeds like there's no tomorrow. There'd better be a tomorrow because we'd like to go home then. Afternoon if we can?'

Jack glanced at Eliza and she nodded. He had no trouble reading Eliza's wordless message that Janice was ready to leave. 'You must take it easy.'

'Janice's mother is staying for a week.' Eliza said. 'I've suggested she shouldn't go home until after her mother's been there for at least a day.'

Janice chuckled softly. 'Peter is a terrific farmer but not much of a housewife. Eliza reckons I'd be better to wait till Mum's had a chance to sort the mess.'

'Sounds like a plan to me. I'll do the newborn check tomorrow morning and see your sutures. If all's well you'll be right to leave after lunch.'

'Thank you.' She lifted her son out of the water carefully and wrapped him in the fluffy towel Eliza had spread out beside the bath. The baby whimpered at the sudden change in temperature but quietened as Janice snuggled him, wrapped tight, up against her shoulder.

Jack caught a look of wistfulness on Eliza's face and stamped down a sudden desire to find out more about his new matron. He hadn't thought that fairy queens went clucky.

Before he could even think about investigating that concept, Eliza had moved on to the two-bed ward and she began to pull the curtains around Keith's bed.

The streaks on Keith's stomach had paled a little but the old man's cheeks were still flushed. 'How's the pain?' Jack was glad to focus on the old man and noted Keith's rapid respirations and elevated pulse rate.

'Not too bad.'

Jack hadn't expected Keith to say anything else but they'd keep a weather eye on him. 'I think we caught the new infection in time, Keith. Hopefully you'll feel better this afternoon. The wound looks a little less angry. I'll leave you in Matron's capable hands.'

'I'll be fine then, Doctor. She doesn't miss much.'

Jack rested his hand on Keith's shoulder. 'So I'm learning.'

'Seems a shame such a good woman isn't married.' Keith winked at Jack who stepped back from the bed as if he'd seen a snake. 'Don't start, old-timer. I'll see you tomorrow.'

They crossed to the other bed and Jack smiled at his patient. 'You've lost the dark circles under your eyes, Joe. I'm glad the pain is more under control.'

'Felt a bit of a wimp.' Joe shrugged his shoulders gingerly with a rueful grin. 'Matron put the wind up me and I have to say the sleep hasn't gone astray.'

'You'll actually get better faster if you have reasonable pain relief,' Jack said. 'Pain is there to tell you something is wrong. Once we know why it's there you don't need to put up with the discomfort any more.'

'That's what Matron said. She's a good woman.' Joe glanced slyly between Jack and Eliza, and Jack had the feeling his able assistant was hard-pressed not to laugh. He admired her for her control. In fact, he admired her far too much for his own peace of mind but it was purely a physical attraction and he knew better than to listen to his libido, or his patients, in his own back yard.

'So, home tomorrow, Joe?' Jack smiled at the younger man's belongings all neatly lined up beside the bed. Joe's hands were out of bandages except for a four-inch strip just past both elbows where the petrol had splashed and burnt the deepest.

'Your fingers are healing well, even though they're pink—that's all new skin growth. You'll have to keep them clean and out of the sun. Remember I told you the new skin has no protection. Lots of sunscreen every couple of hours if you're outside—OK?'

Joe's eyes were shining with anticipation. 'Will do, Doc. My sister will pick me up. She's lending me one of her sons to stay at my place to do the dirty work for the next few weeks.'

'That's great. Stay away from the bush-fires—it looks like we're in for a bad couple of weeks. If fires come your way, you're to pack what you can and come straight back into town and join the sandwich brigade. No firefighting. OK?'

'If you say so, Doc.'

Jack lifted his hand in farewell and glanced at Eliza. He thought she'd paled a little and he narrowed his eyes.

'You OK?'

'Fine,' she said, 'I had a bad experience with a bushfire once, but that was a long time ago.'

'Can I do anything to help?' He'd thought there was something, and she'd looked quite distressed. He followed her out of the room.

She paused and waited for him to catch up, and he caught the drift of her soap, or shampoo, or whatever it was that seemed to linger in his mind after he'd left her.

The scent played havoc with his concentration. Plenty of people smelt like herbal soap, and he didn't take a scrap of notice. Why should she be any different?

Jack frowned his mind back into gear. 'So what happened?'

'I don't want to talk about it. What did you think of Keith's wound?'

He didn't say anything for a moment, just looked at her, and then he shrugged and followed her lead. 'The wound may look better but I'm not happy with Keith. If you're concerned or the night girls get worried, give me a call. If he gets any worse, stop all food and fluids and watch for paralytic ileus. The infection could slow down his gut. We'd have to send him back to Armidale if his bowels shut down, and he doesn't like being that far from home.'

Eliza nodded. 'Keith's worried about Ben, his cattle dog. The neighbour's looking after him but Keith's still fretting.'

'He'll have to wait a day or two longer.'

There was silence as they both contemplated Keith's problem. Jack led the way to the aged wing and they managed a thorough round with time to spare before he was due to start his surgery day. He was consistently surprised how cheerfully Eliza was greeted after only a few days. It seemed the older residents were more than happy with their new matron.

'You seem to have your finger on the pulse here already.'

Eliza rolled her eyes. 'Is that a pun?'

'Definitely.'

She groaned and almost laughed. 'Don't. My father used to tell puns all the time up until...' She stopped and frowned. 'Never mind. Tell all the puns you want, it's your hospital. I'll phone you if we have any worries.'

Eliza watched him go and reminded herself she needed to be careful not to care too much for Jack. He unsettled her and made her feel like blurting things out, and that was something she'd never done—or had even had the opportunity to do. She'd always been the listener, the one who attracted needy people, but suddenly Jack felt like a father confessor. He was opening old wounds she'd had sealed off for years, and it was scary how easily he could do it.

She regretted she'd come here. Then she thought of Mary and how she'd have just kept working on despite her pregnancy with no one to relieve her, and Eliza couldn't wish that back.

She must have ended up here for a reason and she'd guess she'd find out why. She just hoped it wasn't so that Jack Dancer could be emotionally healed at her expense and she'd pay the price again.

'I said, my piles are getting worse, Doctor.'

Jack roused himself from remembering the way Eliza had looked that morning and concentrated on the elderly woman seated in front of him.

'I'm sorry to hear that, Mrs Rowe. Have you been taking those paracetamol and codeine tablets again?'

The elderly lady avoided his eyes. 'I might have had a couple in the last few days, now that you come to mention it, Doctor. Would they hurt my piles?'

'Not directly they won't, but the codeine in the tablets will make you constipated, and all that straining is sure to make your haemorrhoids worse. So something else must be troubling you. Where are you getting the pain?'

'Only in my piles.'

Jack blinked. 'Why are you taking the pain tablets, then?'

'To be honest, Doctor, it's my Jem. His snoring is that loud, I can't sleep. If I pop two of them tablets, I sleep like a baby.'

Jack shook his head. 'I'll give you a prescription for a mild sleeping tablet and ask Jem to come and see me. I'll have a look down his throat and we might see about booking him into a sleep lab for his snoring. He could be having some breath-holding while he's asleep.'

Mrs Rowe sat up and her eyes brightened. 'You wait till I tell Norma. To think my Jem could be sick when he's never had a sick day in his life. Well, I never.' She sat back with a thoughtful expression on her face. 'Would that make him tired? He's always saying he's tired these days.'

'It could.' Jack stood up and handed Mrs Rowe the prescription he'd just printed out on his computer. 'Take one or two of these tablets at night until we sort Jem out.'

Jack came around from behind the polished desk and opened the door for his patient. He suppressed a yawn. Jem wasn't the only one who wasn't sleeping well.

Since Eliza May had come to Bellbrook he was doing some tossing and turning of his own. It seemed a long time until six o'clock tonight and he could go home. Maybe he needed some fairy dust to get to sleep. The thought brought a fleeting smile to his lips until he realised he was grinning like an idiot.

CHAPTER FOUR

IN THE early hours of the morning, Keith's temperature soared. The night sister, Rhonda, concerned and unsure of what to do, rang Eliza to come until the doctor arrived. Jack had been called out to a croupy child.

When Eliza arrived Keith was flushed and muttering as he pulled his sheet over his shoulders and shifted in the bed.

Eliza turned his pillow and tucked the cotton in around the old man's thin shoulders. 'How are you, Keith?' He looked dreadful to her.

Keith squinted one eye open and tried a smile. 'Been better. Thought I saw the Grim Reaper standing beside the bed before.' He was only half joking. His eyes narrowed as he tried to concentrate. 'You're early. Is it morning already?'

'Not quite. Rest and I'm here if you want anything. I'm going to sit beside you until Dr Jack gets back from his callout and can come and see you.'

Keith turned his face fully towards Eliza and weak tears formed at the edges. He grabbed her fingers. 'Don't let him send me away to one of them city hospitals. I don't want to die away from home.'

Eliza squeezed his shoulder with her other hand. 'You're not going to die, Keith, we won't let you. As for being transferred, you know Dr Jack won't transfer you out unless he absolutely has to.'

'If anything happens to me, will you look after my dog, Matron?' The old man's grip tightened on her fingers and she soothed him.

'Nothing is going to happen to you, Keith, but I'll look out for Ben. Now, you rest quietly until these antibiotics can work.'

She eased her fingers out of his grip and wiped the sweat from his weathered face, then increased the intravenous infusion rate to compensate for the fluid loss. Eliza calmed him with her voice. 'Close your eyes and just drift off when you can. I'll natter on in the background so you know I'm here.'

She began to talk softly about her years growing up on her father's farm and the animals she'd had. When he fell into an uneasy sleep her voice fell silent.

As she watched, the old man twitched and turned, and the sweat trickled down his neck onto the pillow. She sponged him and changed his linen as necessary.

Tension mounted in the next hour for Eliza as the old man worsened. The sight of his fevered face brought back the last painful memories of her father.

Eliza had been eighteen and left in charge of the house while her father had fought a fire caused by a lightning strike at the bottom of the paddock. It had been weather similar to what they'd had the last few days and Eliza could still remember the smell of burnt eucalyptus in the air and the crackle of the fire in the undergrowth.

She'd blocked the house gutters and filled them with water and had been hosing the flower-beds around the house when the wind had suddenly picked up. She'd lost sight of her father when the treetop-high wall of fire had jumped the waterhole and engulfed her father, before racing up the hill through the whiskey grass towards her.

She remembered the spurt of water from the hose in her hand as it slowed to a dribble when the pump house was engulfed and killed her water supply.

Fear for her father froze her steps as she watched in horror as the fire came closer, easily devouring everything in its path. Before she had a chance to turn and run for the house she saw the vegetable garden and then the outside toilet catch light, and that was when she was sure she was going to die.

She thought the noise of her heart thumping was deafening even above the sound of the flames, until she realised the noise and vibration was coming closer and louder from above her head.

Suddenly a deluge of cascading water hit the ground in front of her and an inexplicable waterfall slid down the hill, extinguishing the fire front. The water helicopter soared away for a fresh load and Eliza could only stand there amidst the smoke and charred grass and sob towards the spot where she'd last seen her dad. Then she broke into a run.

She found him in the waterhole. At first she thought he'd escaped injury, and externally he had. But the flames and heat had seared his lungs and Eliza clung to his hand while they watched the helicopter douse the last of the runaway flames before coming to land beside them on the paddock.

He was airlifted out of their country town to the city and he never came back. For the two days it took him to die she always assumed he'd return, and never quite forgave herself for surviving when he hadn't.

Usually she avoided thinking about that time because it brought back memories of her own helplessness the last time she'd seen him. Her lack of first-aid knowledge had been one of the main reasons she'd gone into nursing.

Isaac's funeral had also been the last time she'd seen her mother. Their meeting had wounded Eliza for years. Even now she didn't want to think about the bitter words that had flown between them—mostly from Eliza.

That was enough reminiscing for the night, she admonished herself and straightened in the chair. When she looked up, Jack was standing beside her.

He looked so solid and dependable and kind. She was glad to see him. 'You're back?'

He nodded at her obvious question and Eliza sighed with relief.

'How's Keith?' Jack's voice was soft in the dim light and she realised again what a caring man he was.

Eliza rotated her neck to release the kinks and consciously dropped her shoulders to ease the tension. Jack was here now, and it felt good to share the load. 'I'm hoping he's on the mend. He's a little more restful than he was half an hour ago.'

Jack stared and looked at the man shifting deliriously beneath the covers. 'That must have been exciting.'

'Just the sort I don't need,' she said dryly, and even she could hear the underlying tension she'd been making light of. Keith was a worry and she had a sudden urge to seek comfort in some physical way from Jack. Maybe lean her head down onto his chest or let him drape his arm around her shoulder for support.

Thankfully—of course she was thankful—Jack did none of those things and she steered her thoughts away with a report on Keith's condition. Jack stood beside her with his hands jammed into his pockets.

'Keith's temperature has come down a little and the last time I looked at his wound I thought he might benefit from probing to release the pressure.'

Jack nodded. 'Let's have a look, then.'

The next hour saw a slim improvement in Keith's condition and the antibiotics were added to again.

When they'd finished making Keith as comfortable as possible, Rhonda, who'd been hovering nearby, suggested they leave Keith with her while they revived themselves with coffee.

Eliza watched Jack stifle a yawn. She shook her head. 'I'll stay another half an hour but I think he's over the worst now. You should go home. I could ring you if he worsens.'

Jack glanced at his watch. 'You have to work in a few hours, too. We'll both stay and keep each other awake for just a little longer. It's been a busy night,' Jack said quietly, as he and Eliza settled in the tearoom.

'You must be exhausted if you've been out since midnight.'

Jack shrugged and glanced at his watch. 'No more than usual. I find I only need a couple of hours sleep.' He perched on the edge of the table and swung one muscular leg back and forth. Eliza busied herself with the kettle and tried to ignore the way her eyes kept straying towards him.

Jack smiled a blinding I-want-something smile and Eliza stiffened her resolve. She must not become entangled with this man. She could feel the hairs rise on her arms as goose-flesh covered her when her body ignored her sensible thoughts.

He spoke quietly but his voice came out deep and rumbling with interest. 'Tell me about yourself. How are you enjoying Bell-brook so far, Matron May?'

She felt the barriers go up this time. 'I'd prefer it if you didn't call me Matron. It's hard enough getting used to the patients calling me that. I know it's how they addressed Mary so I can't change it. But I get the feeling you're mocking me when you use that form of address.'

He raised his eyebrows. 'I'm far from mocking you.' He paused, and then did as she asked. 'Eliza.' A shiver ran down her neck and suddenly she wished he'd call her Matron again.

'Now you call me Jack.' The odd inflection in his voice made her look up at him.

She didn't answer and he smiled mockingly. 'Coward.' Then he said, 'Eliza is a lovely name. Is it a family name?'

Eliza felt like she was slipping down a hill backwards with this conversation. She couldn't find purchase in her descent into con-fusion. 'It's my middle name.' Eliza shook her head. 'I was named after my mother,

Gwendolyn, but I dislike the name and changed to Eliza when I was eighteen.'

'Does that mean you don't get on with your mother?'

Eliza raised her eyebrows. 'I wouldn't know. I've only seen her once since I was seven.'

There was silence for a few minutes while Jack drank his coffee and digested her comments.

Good, she'd shocked him, thought Eliza as she pulled Keith's patient notes towards her to write up her latest observations.

Maybe Jack would stop asking such personal questions because he was doing dreadful things to her stomach when he looked at her like that.

It seemed not. 'If I've been insensitive, Eliza, it's because I find myself unexpectedly at ease with you, considering our rocky start.'

Eliza's pen skidded across the page in an untidy zigzag as she looked at him in shock. 'Well, you fooled me.'

'Don't worry.' He grinned wryly. 'You're

safe from propositions. I learnt my lesson a long time ago and I'm not looking to find a soulmate this century.'

She couldn't help smiling. 'Well, seeing as it's only early in the century, I doubt you'll live for the next one.'

Jack acknowledged her wall of reserve. He could see the hurt reflection of himself, and it wasn't his job to rescue Eliza from her ghosts. He carried his own burden of loss and he had never forgiven himself for not being there for Lydia. The shell around Eliza rang bells of recognition and he wondered what had happened to make her so wary of opening herself to others.

Maybe he could make the reluctant Eliza laugh.

He persisted. 'So let's be friends. I could do with a Nice Safe Female Friend.'

'Sounds delightful. NSFF. What makes you think I'm safe?' Eliza looked less than impressed with the prospect.

'You told Mary you're off men. I think

you're even less likely to be on the lookout for a marriage proposal than I am.'

He had that right, judging by the vehement nod of her head. 'Correct. The next man who wants to marry me had better fly me to Gretna Green because I'll be kicking and screaming all the way to the altar.'

He felt the same. 'So now that we have that out of the way, tell me what you want to do after you leave Bellbrook. What's your goal in life?'

It was four in the morning and Eliza suppressed a yawn. She probably thought that humouring him would keep her awake.

He watched her frown as she gathered her thoughts. 'I've almost paid off my flat in Randwick. Originally I bought there to be close to my training hospital, and when I'm clear on that I want to buy a mountain hide-away with a few acres and a creek. Somewhere not too far, so I can escape from Sydney on weekends.'

She'd surprised him. 'So you're not a dyed-in-the-wool Sydneysider?'

He wanted more information but she was reluctant. He wondered why she wasn't used to talking about herself. 'We need to get back to Rhonda,' she said.

'Soon,' he said, and didn't move.

'You're persistent,' she said dryly, and he suppressed a smile. He could see her wavering.

Jack lowered his voice, and tried for persuasion. 'Tell me about the man who let you down.' Maybe the softness of his request was a factor, but she answered him.

'Which one?' She looked surprised at herself when she answered.

Jack blinked. 'There's been more than one?'

Eliza shrugged. 'After my father died in a bushfire…' She looked up and he connected that with what she'd spoken earlier, then she went on.

'I had to go to Sydney to live and trained to be a nurse. At uni I met and fell in love with an older man with a tortured past and we seemed to be good for each other.'

'We—mostly he, but I didn't mind—decided

to quietly slip away and get married without telling anyone. Strangely, I thought, he became more distant as the wedding approached. Until the day before the wedding when he called, thanked me for waking him up to life again and said he had fallen for another woman. He became the first of a pattern.'

Jack screwed his face up and shook his head. 'How could you make a pattern out of that? The guy was obviously a jerk.'

Eliza half smiled at his championing. 'My last fiancé, Alex, had been let down by his previous lover and again I thought we suited each other. We became engaged, again he didn't want people at work to know, so it was just between the two of us. Our plans were so much a secret that before we set a date for the wedding he ran off with my unit manager.'

She stared down at her ringless finger. 'I'd actually thought I'd finally found a man who didn't need to work out his psychological problems on me, but Alex capped off a less than inspiring love life. If I tie that to my parents' marriage failure and growing up with my recluse of a father, I have to agree with my psychologist.'

Jack tucked his chin into his chest and stared at her from under his brows incredulously. 'You have a psychologist?'

'Wouldn't you?'

Jack did his wide-eyed goldfish impersonation as he struggled for air, and Eliza swallowed a bubble of satirical laughter. Well, he'd asked for it, Eliza thought grimly. It may as well be all out on the table so he doesn't get any ideas.

'My psychologist says I suffer from disconnection because of my mother's abandonment, which leaves me with diminished self-worth. That's why I fall victim to the needs of others and for men who are emotionally scarred, and can't return unconditional love.'

'Good grief!' A smile tugged at the corner of his mouth and Eliza glimpsed the humour in the telling. It was surprisingly therapeutic to laugh at herself.

Maybe saying this out loud wasn't too bad after all. 'My new goal is to skim through life without love or the danger of wasting energy on another useless man.' She sat back and actually felt lighter than she had for weeks.

Jack scratched his ear. 'Let me get this straight. Your parents broke up and you stayed with your father, so where did you actually grow up?'

'On a farm near Macksville.'

'That's not all that far from here.'

Eliza smiled but didn't comment. 'Dad home schooled me until I was twelve. When I went to high school I found it hard to make friends. The only people who would talk to me were the ones who nobody else would listen to. I became a good listener.' She grimaced and stood up. 'Except when I'm around you, it seems.'

'I'm not bored.'

'Well, I am.' She couldn't believe she'd told

him so much. Eliza picked up the chart from the table. 'Let's relieve Rhonda.'

Jack had been pleased with their new rapport, and found himself even more intrigued by the screwed-up life of Eliza May. She'd left him with a lot to ponder.

When they returned to the bedside, Keith seemed more settled and Rhonda was happier with his condition. She promised to check on him every fifteen minutes for the rest of the night.

Eliza heaved a sigh of relief. 'I'm glad we can manage Keith here, though his wound will keep him in for another two weeks at least. He was worried you'd transfer him out.'

Jack nodded. 'I think he'll improve now. Just dress the wound as often as it's needed and we'll keep him on the IV antibiotics for another week. The sensitivities should be back tomorrow so we'll know if it's the right antibiotics.'

Eliza glanced at the closed curtains across the room. 'It's lucky Joe is going home tomorrow. If we are careful, do you think Joe can still visit Keith without endangering his own wounds?'

'I think he'll be fine.'

She nodded and led the way back to the nurses' station. 'I'll see you in the morning, then.'

'Goodnight, Eliza.'

There was a note in Jack's voice that she hadn't heard before, and it kept her awake longer than she wished when she finally crawled into bed. She'd have to be very careful to maintain her distance.

By the time Eliza had been in Bellbrook for two weeks she'd begun to socialise more. She filled in for the night social tennis with Carla and a group of younger women, but both times she appeared on the court, the next day on the round, Jack had been able to recite the scores and what time she'd gone to bed after the game.

'Do you seek this knowledge or is it forced

on you?' Eliza shook her head at the things people told Jack.

Jack grinned. 'You're big news around here.'

'Only because everyone wants to match-make me with you.' Eliza shook her head in mock-disgust. It was fun to spar with Jack, maybe too much so, and they had to remember the whole town watched them and she at least didn't want them to get the wrong idea.

'I'm a great catch.'

'I can think of lots of catches to hanging around with you. Not interested. Sorry.'

He lowered his voice and leant towards her. 'That's why I enjoy being with you.'

Eliza looked over her shoulder but nobody stood near. That was all she needed—a rumour like that. 'Don't even joke about it.'

October had started warm and grew warmer—as did the rapport between Jack and Eliza. By the fourth of the month the weather was scorching. On the wards the heat was the favourite topic. The elderly were starting to worry about the approaching summer temperatures.

When the first pall of bushfire smoke rose in the hills, most of the patients made their way to the hospital veranda to shake their collective heads and predict disaster.

'The worst I've seen was back in fifty-six,' Keith sighed as he remembered. 'Four lives were lost, two of Jack's uncles and their sons. A whole branch of the family wiped out when they were caught by a wind shift up the wrong end of the gully.'

Joe was in, visiting, and he nodded. 'I wasn't born then but I remember my father talking about it.'

'We've a good man in charge now.' Joe turned to Eliza.

Eliza blinked as she squashed the images of her father and her own brush with death. She hated bushfire season and had sworn she'd never put herself at risk there again. The city, or at least where she lived, didn't have bushfires. Another reason she shouldn't have come to Bellbrook.

'Matron Mary's husband is the fire chief,' Joe went on. 'Mick's had a lot of experience. He flies all over the state as an advisor. He was some big fire chief in the navy.'

By lunchtime the call had gone out for all available men to present to the brigade hall because the wind was pushing the flames down the hills towards the town.

Mary arrived at the hospital, ostensibly because she didn't want to be out at her house alone but really to help Eliza as the first of the minor casualties began to trickle in.

The radio was on in the background in every room and Eliza couldn't escape the updates. 'Thousands of acres lost, cattle dead, shedding and fences lost, but no homes yet.'

'No lives lost, thank goodness.' Keith repeated what was on all their minds.

The outpatient bell rang again as Eliza fixed the nebuliser to the face of their second asthma sufferer and Eliza smiled at Mary hovering beside her.

'You knew it would be like this, didn't you?'

Mary nodded. 'I thought it might. I'll go and see this next one, shall I?'

'Thank you.' Eliza couldn't leave the young girl she was with until she was sure the bronchodilator was going to work, and she suspected Mary was itching to have her hand in. Eliza just hoped Jack wouldn't blame her for Mary's reappearance.

Eliza knew Jack had been called to a house out of town for a middle-aged woman found unconscious by her distant neighbour, and he had to wait for the ambulance to arrive.

The day grew even hotter and a steady stream of elderly citizens arrived to help the residents make sandwiches in the main dining room for the firefighters. All of the volunteers sighed as they entered the air-conditioned coolness of the hospital.

When Jack arrived, Mary had finally been

persuaded to lie down in the office on a folding bed. She'd only succumbed to Eliza's hourly imploring because of the doctor's imminent arrival.

When Jack walked in, order ruled alongside Eliza with all beds full with those she hadn't wanted to discharge home without seeing Jack.

He threw his car keys on the desk. 'Been busy while I was away?'

'Slightly. We've three asthmatic children exacerbated by the smoke, two minor burns, an infant who had a febrile convulsion and one suspected broken wrist from a pushbike altercation with a panicked kangaroo.'

'Good old Bellbrook,' he said with a grin. 'I'll bet Mary is livid she's missing this.'

Eliza met his eyes reluctantly. 'She hasn't missed much. She's been here hands on for most of the morning but I've persuaded her she needs a rest and she's lying down in the office.'

Eliza waited for the explosion but when she

met his eyes Jack was staring down at her quizzically.

'Were you worried I was going to blame you for Mary being here?'

So he could read minds. 'I wondered.'

'Mary is her own boss—which incidentally is why she makes such a good matron. The downside is she's hard to keep at rest when you want her to. I have great confidence you will prevent her from doing anything silly. Am I right?'

'I should hope so.' Eliza felt as though she'd been given a reprieve, which was ridiculous.

Jack seemed to think everything was normal. 'Let's clear the beds, then, shall we?'

They set to and within the hour all the patients had been seen, Eliza's initial diagnoses and treatment confirmed and sent on their way. Most would come back tomorrow for review and/or dressing of the burns, and the fractured wrist was off to Armidale for X-rays.

'You've done well, Eliza.'

She glowed from those few words even though she warned herself she was a fool. 'Thank you, Jack. Mary helped.'

'And the responsibility was with you.' He sat down at the nurses' station. 'Now, the patient I've been with, Dulcie Gardner, is fifty-four and has been transported to Armidale with a mild left-sided stroke. Her condition and prognosis are good with only a little left-sided weakness and slurring of speech. After she is assessed by a neurologist, I'm hoping they'll allow her to convalesce here. One of my distant cousins is an occupational therapist on maternity leave and she'll come in and monitor her progress for the next few weeks. How do you feel about admitting someone long term and initially labour intensive at this time?'

Of course it wasn't a problem. 'Fine.'

He smiled and she wondered just how many times he'd got his own way with that strategy. 'I was hoping you'd say that. But there's more.'

'That serves me right for being eager to

please. You sound like one of those television commercials. And what would the "more" be?'

His dark eyes twinkled at her. 'Are you feeling eager to please?'

'Don't push your luck, Dr Dancer.'

He seemed reluctant to start on his next request but finally got around to it. 'I wondered if you'd consider moving into Dulcie's house temporarily? I know it seems bizarre, but it's a lovely little cottage and it even has a creek. The main problem is Dulcie's menagerie.'

Eliza's eye's widened at the unexpected request but Jack went on.

'The animals in her back yard need feeding twice a day. She's also one of the few people in Bellbrook not related to anyone else, so I can't pull a cousin from somewhere to take over her pets. She has a daughter in Sydney somewhere but they don't talk. It was one of the things Dulcie spoke about before the ambulance came.'

Jack was talking about a house, almost a farm, with animals, to look after on her own? She wasn't sure if she was scared or excited at the thought which surprised her more. 'Why me?'

'Because you're here for the next six weeks or so and she'll probably be in hospital for some of that time at least. I know you hate your bed at the pub and you said you wanted a hide-away.'

He had it all figured out and the pub was driving Eliza batty with the noise on the weekends. It did sound peaceful. 'When did you want me to start?'

He sighed with relief. 'That's great. What about tomorrow afternoon, if you could? The neighbours will sort the animals in the morning. I fed them while I was there this afternoon and all should be fine overnight. There's a donkey, some rabbits and a few hens, as well as a goat or two. I think the cat and dog have enough dry food to last them until tomorrow as well.'

'Good grief! You weren't joking about a menagerie. What makes you think I could handle all those?'

His dark eyes crinkled. 'A farm girl like you? No problem.'

He'd certainly been listening while she'd babbled on that night. Eliza narrowed her eyes. 'And why can't you move in and mind the animals?'

'I have my own dependants and you're one of the few people in town without commitments.' He lowered his voice. 'Dulcie has a real feather bed in her guest room. You'd probably sleep like a baby in that.'

On Tuesday afternoon Eliza packed her few belongings at the Bellbrook Inn and transferred them to Dulcie's tiny cottage five kilometres out of town. It was a dream of a place with a white picket fence, a moon gate above the driveway and a multitude of flowering shrubs.

Jack followed her out in his car to show her

where the feed was and introduce her to Dulcie's animals.

A large cross-cattle dog with mournful eyes and a pretty face licked Eliza's hand as she climbed out of her car.

'Did you send word ahead I was the hand that feeds, Dr Dancer?'

Jack laughed and stepped out of his four-wheel-drive. 'Roxy loves everyone. Not your most reliable watchdog but she did run two kilometres to the neighbours to tell them her mistress was sick.'

That was it for Eliza. 'You clever thing.' She crouched down and hugged the dog, who quite happily licked her face. Eliza pushed her away, laughing. 'I may think you are a hero, Roxy, but don't lick me! I'm here to see everyone. Lead on, sir.'

Jack gestured grandly with his arm. 'Poco, the donkey, is easy as long as you keep the water up to him. The goats graze fairly well, too, and I believe Dulcie divided the scraps between the rabbits and the hens. Goodness knows where the cat is, but I'm sure she will turn up for dinnertime.'

Eliza darted backwards and forwards, peering at animals and doling out food. He smiled at her enthusiasm and Eliza smiled back. She couldn't remember when she'd felt this euphoric despite all the responsibility. Maybe she had missed living in the country.

'When Dulcie comes back from Armidale tomorrow, you'll be able to reassure her so she'll rest more easily.'

Eliza looked at Jack standing there with a grin on his face, as if he didn't have the weight of the town on his shoulders. He was oblivious of the fact that not many doctors would be concerned enough about a patient and her pets to give up a little of the precious free time he had to settle someone in to look after them.

Lately she'd wondered if the town took Jack just a little for granted. 'I know you've put this on me and in the end I'm the one carting water, but it is nice you care, Jack. You're not a bad man.'

He raised his eyebrows mockingly. 'As far as men go, eh?'

Eliza inclined her head. 'As you say.'

'Well, as you said, you'll be the one carrying water. I think you're a champ to take them on.' He glanced around. 'Are you happy with the isolation? I'd forgotten how quiet it is out here. You're not worried about the fires, are you? It's a very clean farm, and the grass in the paddocks is short up to the house.'

Eliza glanced at the mountain behind her and the lushness of the forest that came down to the back boundary in front of the creek. The front paddock had been recently slashed and there was no debris around the house to be a fire hazard. She shrugged. 'It's wonderful. I'm fine. Dad's farm was much more remote.'

Jack nodded. The tension between them slowly built, which was a shame as it had been so easy earlier. Please, don't say anything, Eliza mentally implored Jack as she willed him to go.

'I'll see you tomorrow, then.' Jack paused and looked at her for a moment as if he were going to say something else.

Finally he waved. 'Goodnight, Eliza.'

'Goodnight Jack.' She sighed with relief as she watched him drive away, and she couldn't think of a negative thing about him. 'You'd better watch your heart, Eliza May, or you'll be crying in your soup in another month or two.'

She turned to the animals—ten pairs of eyes staring at her with expectation.

'We are going to have fun, people.'

CHAPTER FIVE

WEDNESDAY morning, Eliza was running late. She'd slept on a cloud with Dulcie's feather bed and had woken after six. Then it had taken twice as long to feed everyone because the donkey had stubbornly refused to move away from the gate so that she'd had to keep climbing over the fence with the three buckets of water.

'Typical domineering male,' Eliza muttered as she poured water in the final trough.

On the way back to the house she remembered the eggs, and by the time she'd watered the hens and collected the eggs it was after seven o'clock.

'I'm sorry I'm late,' she said to Rhonda and Vivian as she hurried in.

Rhonda just smiled. 'Dr Jack rang and said you might be.'

'Oh he did, did he?' Smart Alec.

'Only a little, he said, honest.' Rhonda played down Jack's disloyalty.

Eliza took pity on the night sister's horror that she'd caused a problem for Jack. 'I'll start the animals earlier tomorrow.' She glanced around. 'So how is everybody?'

As Rhonda finished handover report and left, Jack arrived.

Eliza looked happy and relaxed and he shelved his disquiet that he'd bulldozed her into minding Dulcie's animals. Matching Dulcie's need and Eliza's experience on her father's farm and her soft heart—the idea had been too good not to act on. But he'd worried she might be upset by the remoteness.

'Good morning, Eliza. Good morning, Vivian.'

Eliza smiled at him and he could feel the vibration right down to his toes. Hell's bells. She'd always had this effect on him but lately it felt as though he was building up a lethal level of exposure to her.

She was smiling cheekily at him and the sun came out. 'Good morning, Doctor. You're early. Were you hoping to beat me here?'

He felt the width of his own smile and control was harder than he wished. This was way outside his comfort zone and he wondered when his awareness of her had crept up to this level. 'So how did it go with your new extended family?'

He'd tossed and turned most of the night because he'd worried she'd be a little nervous. And then there'd been the feather-bed fantasies.

Eliza was waxing lyrical about her new residence. 'I love it out there. Though I've learnt the meaning of 'as stubborn as a donkey', but apart from Poco, everything went well.'

Their eyes met and the warmth in hers, even though it originated from a donkey and not from him, was a lovely way for him to start the day. But start the day he must. And drag himself away he'd better.

'What time do you think Dulcie will be transferred back?' Eliza queried as she picked up the patient notes.

Eliza had asked him a question—he really needed to concentrate. 'Some time before lunch, I imagine.' He couldn't remember being this scatterbrained when he'd first met Lydia, who was the only yardstick he had. Though, of course, these feelings were nothing like those when he'd fallen for Lydia.

'Well, Vivian and I will finish the rest of our work before she arrives.'

The two of them walked down to see Keith, while Vivian sped off to ensure the seniors were up for breakfast, and Jack remembered the first time he'd strode down the corridor with Eliza. Had it only been a couple of weeks ago?

Jack shrugged off his strangely obsessive behaviour and turned to look at Keith. The old man appeared much more himself and Eliza pulled the curtains.

Jack cleared his throat as if to start his day afresh. 'So you're almost ready for home, too, Keith?'

He could feel Eliza's surprise beside him but she followed his lead.

'If I take the dressing down now, you can see how much the wound has improved,' she said.

Jack nodded and Keith slid down his pillows to let Eliza at the tape.

Keith couldn't believe his luck. 'Are we talking soon, Doc? My dog will have forgotten what I look like.'

'No way Ben could do that.' He peered at the now exposed wound. 'That looks great, Keith. If you'll come in and see me in two days at the surgery, I reckon you can go home today, too. You're to come back here if the fires come close to home. And you can bring your dog. I'm sure we can find somewhere to tie Ben up if we need to.'

The old man's face creased with delight. 'You beauty.'

Jack smiled. 'Your old truck has been waiting in the hospital car park for a few weeks now. I hope it starts.'

Keith swung his legs out of the bed. 'A little thing like that won't stop me.'

As they walked back to the desk, Eliza beamed beside him. She genuinely cared about his patients. 'It's a pleasure to see how keen Keith is to go home. I didn't expect he'd be allowed to go—nor did he.'

Jack's face was serious. 'I've been out to see Mary's husband, Mick. He seems to think we're in for a bad run with the fires over the next few days. I thought it better that Keith got home to see things were right before it was too late.'

Eliza felt the dread in her stomach. 'What about Dulcie's farm?'

'I asked about that and Mick said the main risk is going the other way. The creek is a good break for Dulcie's too, but Mick will keep it under surveillance.' He glanced around at the quiet hallway. 'I think you're going to need all your hospital beds before we're through.'

'What about Mary's pregnancy? She only has ten days to go.'

At least Eliza understood. He was having an uphill battle getting through to Mary. 'That's the reason I was out at the McGuiness farm.' He ran his fingers through his hair. 'I want her in Armidale, at least until after the baby is born. I'm not that sure of her due date because she wouldn't go for a scan. Has some aversion to ultrasounds. So I hope this baby is fine. But if things get worse she's better here than home alone. We'll just have to keep her sitting down as a triage nurse or something.'

'I'll watch her.'

'I know you will.' He glanced at his watch. Eliza was good in the common-sense department and a couple of other departments he wished he had more time for. 'I'll scoot off and start surgery. I might even have my secretary double up the appointments so I can finish early. I'm not usually superstitious but I have a bad feeling about today.'

Dulcie Gardner arrived at eleven and settled into the ward smoothly. She could stand upright with help but had difficulty walking without assistance and her words were slightly slurred. She was improving so rapidly there was every chance she would return to full health as long as she gave her body the time it needed to recuperate.

'So you're the new matron who's minding my family?' Dulcie's medical records may have said she was fifty-four years old but she looked forty-four, with her wavy blond hair and pale blue eyes. Her smile was dragged down at one side but still quite lovely, and Eliza warmed to her at once.

'Hello, Dulcie. Yes, I'm Eliza and all your

family are delightfully well and waiting for you to get better.'

'How was the bed? Did you find the sheets?'

Eliza smiled as she began to pack Dulcie's things away in the drawers. 'Your guest room has a much better bed than the one in the Bellbrook Inn.' Eliza put away powder and soap and combs and a hair drier and even found a little travel clock to put on the locker.

'You seem to have everything, considering you were whisked away in the ambulance.'

'Dr Jack packed for me. I swear that man is an angel.'

He is a good man, Eliza agreed silently. 'He was certainly worried about your animals.'

Dulcie bit her lip. 'Because I said I wasn't going if he didn't find someone to move in with them until I come home.'

Eliza smiled at the thought of Jack at a stalemate with this lovely lady. 'I'd like to have seen that.'

'Perhaps I was a little ungrateful to give him

such a hard time, but I can be stubborn.' Dulcie looked apologetically at Eliza and Eliza squeezed her hand.

'Your donkey was stubborn this morning and wouldn't move from the gate. He must have got it from you, or perhaps you got it from him? I had to climb over the fence to fill the water troughs because he wouldn't move.'

Dulcie hiccoughed with laughter. 'I forgot to tell Dr Jack you have to give him an apple to move.'

They shared a smile. 'Well, no more worry about that. You did what you needed to keep your family safe.' She lowered her voice conspiratorially. 'It would do Dr Jack good not to get his way all the time. I fear he's a little spoiled by the adoration that goes on here.'

'I beg your pardon' Jack's voice held a thread of amusement so Eliza was saved from embarrassment. He didn't look at Eliza as he crossed to his patient.

'Hello, Dulcie. You look better already since the last time I saw you.'

'I am, Dr Jack. They looked after me well but it is good to be home. And I approve of our new matron.'

'She's a bit of a tyrant, though,' Jack said, as if Eliza wasn't there. 'I saw the ambulance pull up and thought I'd duck my head in to see how you travelled. You make sure she looks after you.'

'You don't need to worry. We girls have it all under control,' Dulcie said with the utmost confidence.

By lunchtime the smoke was strong enough in the distance to seep into the hospital and Eliza could feel the old dread return to her stomach.

Mary was ensconced as triage nurse and seemed content to do paperwork and initial observations and otherwise keep her weight off her feet.

Any outpatients who came in brought the

smoky smell in their clothes and hair. The sun had disappeared behind the haze in the pitiless sky.

The seniors were busily assembling sandwiches again and the volunteers were filling flasks with water and juice and gallons of tea. The radio was informing listeners where backburning operations were taking place and the quarter-hourly updates had everyone's attention.

At one o'clock, the sound of a truck heralded the arrival of two new helpers and one blue cattle dog.

When Eliza looked up she knew things were getting worse. 'That must be the shortest discharge in history, Keith.'

'Joe was in a spot of bother and I thought we should come back.'

Later Eliza found out that Keith had driven over to Joe's farm and had found his young friend trapped back against the wall of his shed. Joe had been trying to hose back the flames of a grass fire caused by floating embers.

Joe's nephew had gone home to help his mother fight their own fire, and though Joe had never intended to become involved in fire-fighting he hadn't been able to stop himself.

When Keith had arrived they'd saved the shed but decided to block the gutters and fill them with water and then leave for town before the road was cut.

Keith's farm was safe and Ben was in the back of the truck.

'We've come to help. Reckon Doc would be spittin' if we both got sick again.'

'I think he might be at that,' Eliza grinned and pointed them towards the day-room where the sandwich factory was still going.

She watched them go and they passed Jack bearing a tray of sandwiches for the staff.

'It seems you may not get much of a break today,' he said, and Eliza felt the jolt right through her at the warmth in his expression. She finally acknowledged how much they enjoyed each other's company, how often they smiled and looked at each other and how dangerous it had all become. Why hadn't she seen this earlier?

She was a fool. 'Let's not waste time chatting, then,' she said, to hide her sudden self-consciousness, and Jack frowned.

Eliza admitted to herself it had been a less-than-gracious thing to say—but it was his fault for getting personal. He'd said she'd just stay a Nice Safe Female Friend but this wasn't the way you looked at friends. She didn't want warm looks on a day that hit one hundred degrees Fahrenheit—she didn't want them ever!

Eliza needed a minute to herself because for some reason she felt like crying. 'Perhaps you should go and see Mary. If she's fine, I'm ready to go through these admissions with you,' Eliza said in a neutral voice.

'Bossy.'

'That's why I make a good boss.' She used his rationale for Mary against him and he went.

* * *

Mary looked up as he approached and Jack thought her shoulders drooped more than normal. 'You're tired, Mary. Have a sandwich and then go and lie down.'

'You sound like Eliza.'

'Heaven forbid.' He smiled with genuine amusement and Mary had to smile back, albeit tiredly. 'OK, so maybe I am a little sore. My back aches and I'm frustrated by not being able to help.'

'You are helping. But you won't help by getting sick or going into labour and not telling me. How long has your back ached for?'

'Most of the pregnancy. Just more notice-able the more weight I'm carrying.'

Jack wasn't convinced. 'Make sure that's all it is. If you go into labour here, I want you out of Bellbrook if I have to carry you myself.'

He jammed his hands into his pockets to keep them from waving around because what he wanted to do was pick Mary up and put her in a car. He'd already lost one woman and his precious baby and he couldn't bear to lose another. Not that anything was going to happen to Mary, he assured himself, but he'd tell Eliza to watch her like a hawk.

'I'm going to ring Mick and get him to come and get you.'

Mary shook her head. 'Mick can't leave the fire control centre. I'll ring Mick's cousin to come over from Armidale as soon as I think I'm going into labour, I promise. I've another ten days to go, and that's if I don't go overdue, which most women do.'

She sounded so reasonable but… 'I don't like it, Mary. I can't force you to go home but I would like you to go as soon as Mick can get away.'

'All right, Jack. Stop worrying about me and go and help Eliza. She has a list of patients to see and will need the beds before you get through the backlog.'

'Two bossy women, and to think, this used to be such a peaceful place.'

As he turned back through the doors he heard Mary say, 'You were in rut anyway.'

'I liked my rut,' he muttered, and went back to Eliza.

By the end of the day Eliza was feeling both the weight of the hospital and the weight of her growing feelings for Jack on her shoulders. Jack had been called out again. On the plus side, the fires were almost under control for the moment, and the gush of outpatients had slowed down.

She'd sent Mary home with her husband at three o'clock and by six Eliza was watching for Jack. She had responsibilities now and had to get home and feed the animals before dark.

They had three inpatients besides the seniors, Dulcie with her stroke; Connie, a young asthmatic child who was almost but not quite well enough to go home; and a new postnatal mum and baby, Cynthia and Liam.

Liam was Cynthia's third child and she'd

only planned to stay overnight for a rest before the fires started. Because she was going home to an isolated farm with no transport, Jack wanted Cynthia to stay until the danger settled.

Jack breezed in about ten past six and had finished the round by half past. Rhonda came in early and Eliza was able to get away not long after Jack. Her shoulders ached and she smelt of smoke and charcoal from all the firefighters she'd ministered to that day.

The animals greeted her enthusiastically and helped her mood a little as she went around and shared the feed. After her shower she couldn't settle, though. She was overtired and agitated and decided a late night from a few nights ago had probably caught up with her—that and her growing unease about her feelings for Jack.

She'd been at Bellbrook over two weeks and it felt like she'd been here for months. It felt like she'd known Jack for ever.

'Well, don't forget you are leaving,' she

reminded herself out loud, and wondered why she should feel even more depressed.

The fires, too, brought many painful memories and she could feel the tension creeping up her shoulders and into her heart.

Since moving to Sydney she'd avoided dwelling on bushfires, changing channels if covered on the TV or the subject when discussed by others.

But here bushfire news was all around her and she couldn't shut it out. Maybe it was time to at least learn to accept that natural disasters were a fact of life.

When the sound of Jack's vehicle penetrated her misery she wasn't sure if she was glad or sorry—she just knew that it would have been better if he hadn't come.

'Hello, Eliza.' He stood tall and a little unsure of his welcome, and she waited for whatever excuse he'd thought up for being here.

'No excuses—I'm here to see you.' He shrugged and she shivered at the thought of how easily he could read her mind and how most of her response leant towards being glad he was there.

'Come in.' She turned away because she didn't want him to read anything else, especially stuff she hadn't even told herself, but she felt the heat in her cheeks as he followed her inside.

He didn't pretend so why was she? Because she wasn't that brave—she wanted to imagine she was immune to Jack.

She sat down in the tiny lounge room and he sat in the chair opposite. No words had passed between them as he'd followed and the silence lengthened as each waited for the other to start.

Eliza couldn't stand the tension any longer. She spread her fingers stiffly across the arm of the chair as if to stop her fists from clenching. 'Why are you here, Jack?'

He looked at Eliza sitting there, her chin lifted as she looked at him with those big, green, fairy eyes of hers, daring him to give a reason for her to throw him out.

He liked her even more for that attitude, but it threw him. What was it he wanted? Why was he here when he'd spent the whole trip out telling himself he was a fool for going near her out of hospital hours?

'I knew you were worried about the fires and I thought I'd just come out and see that you were OK.'

'I'm fine. Thank you. It was kind of you to think of me.'

'I think of you a lot.'

She sighed. 'It's a problem we both seem to have.'

'I guess you're feeling it, too, then,' he said quietly. He watched her close her eyes briefly as she took a deep breath, and then she was back to her assertive self.

'It doesn't matter what I feel, Jack. I'm leaving soon. I've been attracted to the wrong man too many times to listen to you about feelings.' Her eyes skittered away and then back again, and he considered that tell-tale sign of her discomfort. There might be some hope.

'At least you admit you're as attracted to me as I am to you.'

'That's not what I said.'

'I just want to find out what there is between us. Maybe there's nothing at all. You said we could be friends.'

Her shoulders rose and then fell. 'I was wrong.'

'I never took you for a coward, Eliza.' He kept his eyes on her and she didn't flinch.

'That's the second time you've called me a coward. I'm not—and I'm not a fool. I wish you hadn't come and I think you'd better leave.'

'No country hospitality?'

'No.'

Maybe there was distress in her eyes, he wasn't sure, but he didn't like the feeling it gave him that he had caused her pain. Maybe he shouldn't have come. 'OK, Eliza.

Perhaps you're right. I'll see myself out and you tomorrow.'

Driving home, Jack was in no better state of mind. He liked Eliza, he really did. And he admired her work and her kindness and he even vaguely understood her crazy mixed-up psyche a little. But it was that look in her eyes that drove him to question his real feelings.

From somewhere, all sorts of protective urges were surfacing and a few of them concerned wrapping her safely in his arms. Maybe it was time he moved on from celibacy. That was all his feelings for Eliza were—biology. His lip curled. There was that but it wasn't a fraction of the whole picture.

He wanted all of her and he was terrified. The last time he'd felt this way he'd been the recipient of more pain than he could stand. He'd reached a point where it had been better to lock Jack the man away and just concentrate on the outside world.

The long hours at the hospital and being out

on call had been a blessing and the responsibility for the health of a town had stopped him from dwelling on any thoughts of a new life. Then Eliza had arrived and pointed her wand at the neat brick wall around his heart and turned it into vapour.

And she was nothing like he'd imagined he'd ever be drawn to. She was bossy, determined, very efficient and probably didn't need him at all. Here he was, fantasising about a woman he'd worked with for less than three weeks. And if he pursued her, if he ever had her returning his feelings, for all he knew, he might let her down like he'd let Lydia down.

So he should give up. Shouldn't he? But those damn eyes of hers were there every time he shut his own. Peace was hard to find.

CHAPTER SIX

THE next day at the hospital was a little quieter as if people were too busy to get sick. The bushfires were closer to town and a pall of smoke lay across the horizon.

After all the soul-searching she'd done the previous night, Eliza wasn't up to discussions with Jack.

When he'd gone he'd still been everywhere in the room. She'd got up and moved into the kitchen but he'd been there, too, even though he hadn't set foot in the tiny alcove.

She'd pushed open the back door and stepped out into the yard. Roxy had bounded up and licked her knee and they'd gone for a walk in the dark. She'd needed to blow Jack

Dancer out of her mind but it had been too dangerous to say it out loud, even to the dog.

Now, twenty-four hours later, she managed to get through Jack's final round by agreeing with everything he said, until she felt like one of those fake nodding dogs in a car rear window.

Eliza stared out the window as Jack finished the baby check on Liam. 'So you agree with that, too?'

Eliza turned back, smiled vacantly and nodded.

Jack's lips twitched and Eliza narrowed her eyes. She searched for any memory of his words but couldn't find any.

'What did I just agree with?'

'That you haven't listened to a word I've said for the last half an hour and I bore you silly.'

Eliza's eyes glinted. 'Yep. I agree with that.' Jack just smiled and handed her the pin for Liam's nappy.

'I'll leave Liam for you to finish dressing then, and head home for my tea.'

Jack out of her hair at last. Eliza nodded. 'Sounds perfect.'

On Eliza's drive home the hazy afternoon sun grew dark in patches. There had been extensive backburning and some areas still smouldered. Eliza switched on her headlights to improve vision as she crawled along the side of the hill. She saw more wildlife than she had the previous evening. Smoke swirled unexpectedly every few hundred yards, a bit like thoughts of Jack in her head, she thought grimly.

Five minutes later Eliza edged her vehicle over for an approaching car and as she squinted to reduce the glare from the other car's headlights, a large marsupial shape bounded out of the bush on her left. The big male kangaroo darted left and then right in fright as the two cars approached, and finally froze in the middle of the road with indecision.

Eliza slammed on her brakes and swerved between the big kangaroo and the high left bank with millimetres to spare. She heard the snap of her side mirror and she winced as it was wiped from the side of her car and branches slapped the paint on her passenger door. Luckily she managed to pull over without hitting the bank with her bumper.

When her car stopped she whooshed out her breath, turned off the engine and sank back against the seat. That had been too close to hitting the kangaroo. She wouldn't like to have been driving fast.

When she played back the scene in her mind unease crawled around the edges of her memory. Something was missing.

It was quiet as she thought about it and then she realised.

The other car had been travelling at a much greater speed and it would have been hard for the driver not to have swerved close to the drop.

Eliza looked back up the way she'd come but there was no car to be seen. She peered further down the road in the opposite direction and a patch of clear in the dusky smoke showed no car.

Eliza swung her wheel tightly and turned the Mustang in a half-circle to face the other direction and crawled slowly up the road and around the bend. She leaned out the window to look at the gravel edge and, as she drew level with where the animal had crossed, she saw the skid marks leading to the rim of the ravine.

Not good. Eliza pulled up, switched on her hazard lights to warn approaching traffic and climbed out of her car.

The tyre marks disappeared short of the low fence and then reappeared as a swathe of broken scrub before careering down the hillside.

She needed help before she attempted to find the occupants because the least helpful scenario would be for her to injure herself in a climb down the ravine, and no one knew she was there. This was not the sort of country where passing drivers noticed a broken branch or two and investigated.

She dialled the emergency number, notified the police and ambulance then went back to her car for a torch and her first-aid kit.

The kangaroo had disappeared and Eliza glared in the general direction in which the marsupial would have escaped.

'Good one, Skippy,' she muttered, and scrambled through the undergrowth at the side of the road to climb the wire fence that the car had managed to sail over.

When she was on the other side of the fence she could see the black marks disappearing down the slope where the tyres had ripped through the soft soil as the driver had tried to brake.

Her shoes were not designed for mountain trekking and she skidded when she couldn't grab bushes to slow her descent. She tightened her lips in sympathy for what must have been going through the mind of the driver in the un-controlled descent.

Finally she picked up the car by way of a glint of metal, but lost her footing as she took her eye off the hillside to examine the wreckage. The last twenty feet she accom-plished faster than she'd intended but managed to land at the bottom still on her feet.

She stopped because she bumped into the rear of what she could now see was a red sports car, and she pulled herself through the bushes at the side of the vehicle until she came to the passenger door.

She reefed the door open and the interior light came on, but the car was empty. There was blood on the steering-wheel but whoever had been in there had managed to get out in case the car blew up.

Eliza looked around and spotted the outline of a woman as she sat upright against a tree.

'Are you all right? I'm a nurse.' Eliza didn't want to frighten her.

Eliza shone the torch onto the woman's chest, careful not to blind her, but suddenly it didn't matter. The woman fainted and that was when Eliza saw she was heavily pregnant. She slid slowly sideways in an ungainly heap and Eliza scrambled across to stop her head, at least, from hitting the ground.

Eliza rolled the woman's weight slightly to one side and tried to elevate her legs onto a log to send more blood to the brain, but she didn't rouse when Eliza spoke to her.

The unconscious woman's breathing was slowing and her pulse was more difficult to palpate than Eliza had expected. She felt the coldness of dread creep over her own body.

In the distance, the sound of an ambulance could be heard, and Eliza hoped they would hurry because she had a horrible suspicion internal injuries were draining the mother's life away. If the mother died the baby would die, too, unless they were somewhere they could perform a miracle.

The next fifteen minutes seemed to last for hours though they extricated the woman more easily from the ravine than Eliza could have hoped for via a lower farm gate. The ambulance had been able to drive along the valley floor and back up to the road in half the time it would have taken to carry the patient out up the slope.

Just as the ambulance drew up to the hospital the cardiac monitor suddenly squealed in protest. The woman's heart had stopped.

'Cardiac arrest.' Eliza felt dread in her stomach and connected the bag to the tube the paramedic had inserted when they'd first arrived. Eliza and the paramedic began CPR but both knew that even the best resuscitation wouldn't be enough for the baby, or the mother, if they didn't stop the internal bleeding.

Jack met them as they opened the doors and took the situation in at a glance. He was relieved and grateful to see they had positioned a wedge under the patient's side and had an intravenous line in.

Jack listened as Eliza reeled off what she knew as they pushed the ambulance trolley into the mini-theatre and transferred the woman onto the emergency bed with barely a break in the cardiac massage.

After two shocks and a dose of cardiac stimulants there was no discernible improvement in the woman's cardiac output. Jack shook his head.

'If you guys continue the CPR,' Jack spoke to the ambulancemen, 'Eliza and I will do the section.'

'Caesarean section? What? Here?' The ambulance officers were astounded but Eliza had heard of this before to save pregnant trauma victims.

Jack knew what had to be done. 'We'll worry about infection if she survives. If we don't get that baby out, Mum has no chance, and without a live mother the baby will die as well.'

Jack turned his focus back to the woman and Eliza drew a deep breath. So be it. She knew it was true. 'Even if it's too late for the baby, we could save her doing this. We'll lose her anyway if we don't try. What do you need, Jack?'

'Everything, but we'll waste time getting it. We both need gloves for our own safety and I'll make a vertical incision. I'll need a scalpel, some antiseptic and a blanket for the baby. If she survives, we'll worry about antibiotics and sewing up later.'

'Should I listen for foetal heartbeats?'

Jack looked at Eliza. 'We don't have time. This is the best chance both of them have.'

During the next three minutes Eliza felt as if she were looking down at the scene from a distance somewhere up on the ceiling, although her body responded as she told it to.

'No anaesthetic—get her belly exposed,' Jack was firing orders. Eliza grabbed a packet of gloves and spoke over her shoulder.

'Rhonda, get the gear ready for the baby. It feels about full-term size and I'll help you when we have her or him.'

Jack knew he had to get the baby out fast. He'd read all the literature and agonised over the might-have-beens with regard to his own personal tragedy. The amazing thing was, there was a very slim chance he could still save this woman's life if he could deliver the baby and get the sequestered blood from her uterus and legs back into her bloodstream by unsquashing the bulky weight of her uterus from the large blood vessels below.

There wasn't much hope, he knew that too, but the woman had none if they didn't try. If any one knew about this scenario, Jack did. If Lydia had been sectioned as soon as she'd arrested, they might have saved her and his son. Or maybe not. He'd never know. But this woman would have every chance he could give her.

'She can sue me later for the scar,' Jack muttered to himself as Eliza poured the contents of a bottle of antiseptic over the pale stomach that seemed so huge on such a tiny woman.

The scalpel swooped and a thin red line appeared beneath the woman's breasts down to the top of her pubis. This wasn't the time for a bikini cut.

Jack slashed again, deeper this time, and he saw Eliza wince as she held open the wound with a large pad. There was very little bleeding as the woman's uterus appeared beneath the slack abdominal muscles and Jack continued doggedly until a gush of amniotic fluid heralded their entrance into the baby's space.

Jack captured the baby's head and then eased the rest of the baby's limp body out of the cavity. Eliza clamped and cut the cord, suctioned and then took the little girl from him. The baby was white and limp and Eliza hurried over to the bench where Rhonda waited with a warm towel and the resuscitation equipment.

Eliza rubbed the little girl briskly as soon as

she'd laid her down, and then tilted the baby's head slightly. Rhonda looked terrified.

Eliza talked her through it. 'For newborns you always start with five slow, bigger breaths with the baby-sized ventilaton bag to force out any fluid from the baby's lungs. This allows better inflation if she starts to breathe for herself. If you don't expel that first fluid, it prevents severely depressed infants from being successfully resuscitated.'

'The baby looks dead,' Rhonda whispered. She'd had very little experience with babies. 'Shouldn't we listen for a heartbeat?'

'You don't have to. Just feel the umbilical cord for any pulsation, but the breaths are the important thing in the first few seconds.' Eliza watched the little chest rise and fall as she squeezed the bag. 'Air entry looks good. There's no heart rate I can pick up so you start cardiac compression. Circle the chest with your hands and use your thumbs over the sternum just under the nipple line. Compress like this for about a third of the depth of the chest.' She showed Rhonda quickly. 'We should have about ninety heartbeats and thirty breaths in one minute.'

They settled into the three compressions of the tiny chest to one smaller breath from the oxygen bag, which was needed for circulation.

The baby twitched and Eliza felt the first flicker of incredulous hope in her own chest. 'Come on, baby. If you're going to do it, it has to be in the next minute or two.' Eliza prayed this baby was as resilient as she knew most babies were. 'Babies want to live,' she said to Rhonda, but she was really talking to herself. 'They are designed for sometimes rocky starts.'

The baby gave a tiny gasp and then another, and Eliza paused in her bagging to check for a heart rate. She could feel the tiny pulsations and the beat speed was climbing fast.

'You can stop compressions, Rhonda, we only need to concentrate on the oxygen now.'

When the baby gave a weak cry, Eliza felt

the tears prickle behind her eyes, but there was no time for emotion. Rhonda straightened in shock and Eliza disconnected the bag from the oxygen tubing and held it near the baby's mouth. The feeble cries grew louder until there was no doubt that she would survive.

The baby settled into a more consistent breathing pattern and after another thirty seconds Eliza glanced across at Jack. 'You go, girl,' she said, and then looked across at Rhonda.

Rhonda was unashamedly crying. 'I can't believe we just did that.'

'I need you here,' Jack called over his shoulder and Eliza nodded to the nurse beside her. 'Keep her warm and keep the oxygen blowing about an inch above her mouth.'

She moved back to Jack, and he nodded congratulations at her success. 'The placenta is out and I've packed the uterus. We can take the wedge out from under her now that the weight of her uterus has gone.'

The ambulance officer stuttered in shock. 'W-we've got the b-beginnings of a heart rate here, if we can keep it going.'

Eliza couldn't believe it. She'd never expected to save both the mother and baby. 'Could she make it, too?' she asked Jack, and he nodded.

'She'd better. We've just given her the best chance we can.'

Jack was grimly determined now there was hope. He mightn't have been able to save his own family but their lives hadn't been wasted if he saved others from what he'd learnt. He wasn't going to let this patient slip away from him.

With a steady heart rate they could run in the needed fluids and the litres of O-positive blood that were arriving from the Red Cross fridge. The woman's heart rate on the monitor was settling down and, although she was still deeply unconscious, her oxygen saturations were creeping up.

'We'd better get some suture material here

and repair this wound so they can airlift her out to a city hospital.'

The next hour saw the arrival of the adult retrieval team in the emergency helicopter and Jack's shoulders sagged as his patient's care was transferred to the new crew.

'Amazing job,' the intensive care doctor congratulated the Bellbrook team, and Eliza and Jack smiled tiredly.

After the police had been, Jack drove Eliza to her car and the silence stretched between them.

Finally Jack spoke. 'This is when I hate being the only doctor in town. I couldn't have done it without you.'

'You were incredible—so focussed on what needed to be done. I still can't believe the mother and baby survived, but I never want to do that again.'

'Tell me about it. She only looked about thirty and we still don't know her name.' They'd pulled up beside Eliza's car.

The sky lit up with a flash of sheet lightning and the slow rumble of thunder followed soon after. Rain would help put out the fires and the break from the heat would be good.

Jack looked mentally and physically exhausted and Eliza didn't feel much better. But she didn't want him to leave her.

'Follow me back to Dulcie's, Jack. Just for a while. I don't want to be alone just now and I don't think you should be either.'

He didn't take his eyes off the steering-wheel as he waited for her to get out, then he nodded, and she heard him sigh.

'It's a strange old world,' he said.

A short time later they both turned off their engines and Roxy greeted them at the gate.

'Yes, I know I'm late,' Eliza said, as Roxy proceeded to cover her in wet doggy kisses. 'And don't lick me.'

Jack smiled faintly at that and Eliza thought it almost worth the dampness to see his spirits lift. 'Come inside,' she said. 'I'll check the animals with a torch later. I filled all the troughs this morning and they'll last until I get to them.'

'I think if I went to sleep I'd never wake up.' Jack followed her into the house and fell into the armchair in the lounge room. His arms hung limply over the sides and she watched him for a moment. His hair was tousled and his skin was paler than usual. 'I'll make us a cup of tea,' she said quietly.

A sudden weight on his chest roused Jack and he realised Dulcie's cat had jumped up. He pushed the cat down onto his lap and stroked it absently.

Life was strange.

If the woman today had been Lydia, if he could have saved his wife and their baby, would their marriage have been different? His son would be three years old now and he didn't suppose that grief would ever go.

But had he really been at fault for the breakdown of their marriage and ultimately Lydia's and his son's deaths?

It was time to let go. He really had loved his wife in the beginning. But she'd been harder to love when she'd become bitter. He'd wanted his baby, ultimately more than Lydia had, but he hadn't known pregnancy would ruin their marriage. He'd actually thought it a wonderful surprise when Lydia had told him.

He'd tried to be there for her. Not work such long hours. But she'd really only been happy when she'd been in Sydney. Goodness knew what sort of mother she'd have been. Perhaps he'd be going through a messy divorce, child access problems. He'd never know.

But Lydia's death, and his son's death, had not been in vain. Because of them he'd known what had to be done today, and another woman and her baby would live.

He and Eliza had done a good job. So had Rhonda and the ambulance officers. They had all achieved an amazing feat.

He could hear the kettle whistle in the kitchen. Eliza was in there. He wished Eliza was here. Now. In his lap instead of the cat.

'Sorry, cat!' He grinned at the purring animal and gently pushed her off so he could stand up.

He followed the kettle's whistle into the tiny kitchen.

Eliza didn't turn as he came into the kitchen. He trapped her against the sink as she put cups on a tray. 'The kitchen's too small for two, Jack. I'll bring the tea out.'

'There's more room if we stand like this.' He took the cups from her hands and pulled her around and into his arms until her nose was buried in his chest.

Her body felt soft and luscious beneath his hands and his fingers tightened on her wrists as he closed his eyes. He dropped his chin down onto the top of her head. Her hair smelt like smoky citrus and he sighed as he relaxed. She felt so good in his arms.

Eliza frowned. 'Right,' she said, and pulled her

head back with a touch of impatience. Her mind was full of what she could whip up for dinner and she missed the change in Jack's focus.

When she tried to step back she realised he still had hold of her wrist. 'What are you doing, Jack?' Then she looked up and saw the expression in his deep brown eyes and unexpected heat hit her low in the stomach like a kick from the donkey.

He just held her, and held her, for several minutes, and it *was* wonderful to rest her head against him and draw comfort from his arms. Then his mouth came down in slow motion and when his lips grazed hers she couldn't help but sigh into him. She needed this and by the feel of Jack against her, he needed her, too.

What started as a gentle comfort kiss slowly deepened into something much more. Strong, slow strokes from his tongue, mirrored by his hands on her body and her hands on his, ignition of flames that had been simmering below the surface for both of them. Suddenly there was no 'both', no 'two people', there was only mutual hunger and a raging desire to oust their shared demons.

When Jack's pager went off, it took a few seconds for him to realise what the sound was. It took Eliza even longer and he had to hold her away until she opened her eyes.

They stared at each other and neither could believe the state of undress they'd achieved in so short a time.

Eliza brushed her hand over her mouth and took a deep breath. 'You'd better answer the page.' Then she turned back to the sink and leant over the cold metal to breathe the fresh air coming through the window.

Jack stared at the back of her neck. Her skin was still pink from where his hand had cupped her, and her white lace bra hung loosely open at the back. He shook his head and picked his shirt up from the floor then went into the other room to phone the hospital.

He'd never behaved like that in his life before. It was as if someone else had shifted into his body and demanded he kiss Eliza, and once he'd started he hadn't been able to stop. She was his oasis in the madness of today but he'd almost created a bigger madness with his lack of control.

His fingers shook slightly as he dialled the number on his phone.

When he came back all traces of the lover had gone and his face was expressionless. 'One of the firefighters, a cousin of mine, is badly injured an hour from town. They don't think he'll make it if they move him so I'm going up to stabilise him before the chopper comes in.'

She nodded and even had the presence of mind to thrust two bananas and a carton of juice into his hand. 'You have to eat something.' He headed for the door but then he stopped again and turned around.

'Eliza.' He shook his head as if unable to find the words, and she made it easy for him.

'Later, or not at all. It's been a big day, Jack, and yours will be even bigger. Good luck.'

Eliza watched him go and she stood looking out of the door as his car receded into the distance. What the heck was she doing? They'd been practically naked in the kitchen and she could guess what would have happened next. Unless he'd pulled a condom out of his pocket in a stellar example of self-control, she could have been pregnant and regretting this day for ever.

Or would she have? Did circumstances cause situations like this or were they just excuses? If she hadn't cared about Jack, deep down, would she have been in this position?

She was way too close to the edge of falling for Jack and she needed to get a grip or leave town, now. Leave Jack before she found herself loving another man who needed healing. But she was trapped until Mary had her baby.

The soft, easily suckered side of Eliza whispered that maybe if he admitted to loving her she could think of them together with a glimmer of hope. But she was scared. Rightly so. She'd thought she'd been in love before—although she'd never experienced the intensity or reckless abandon she'd felt in the last few minutes. But that had probably just been exacerbated by the horrific drama of the day.

She'd just have to see what the next day brought but the glow remained.

CHAPTER SEVEN

'I THINK it would be better if we didn't mention that I called out to see you at Dulcie's,' Jack said. 'Just for a while.'

She froze and the morning round shattered into reality. Another 'secret' relationship.

Her face felt stiff as she struggled to keep it bland and fight down the sudden nausea that gripped her.

'Why is that, Jack?'

He leant on the desk as he looked at her and he frowned. 'Just don't, OK?'

Eliza stared at this stranger she'd probably given her heart to. Was he going to give her a reason or tell her he wasn't regretting last night? But, of course, he didn't. She couldn't believe how much of a fool she'd been. Again.

She'd seen this one coming. She'd opened herself to this risk and look where it had left her. Next-morning regrets from a man who should have grown out of them.

Not that she'd planned to shout their attraction from the rooftops but a look or a touch of his hand on hers at work, celebrating a new closeness, would have been good to her. Second thoughts and secret relationships were something she'd vowed never to settle for again.

Regrettably, she couldn't leave today. She'd ring Julie, though, and get the agency moving on looking for a replacement. It could take weeks to get away but she could be strong for that long.

Jack behaved as if nothing had happened, and Eliza supposed she had actually given him the opportunity to do exactly that when she'd said to him 'Later, or not at all,' in Dulcie's kitchen. But she hadn't thought he'd take her up on it.

Eliza would have to be thankful that she'd woken up to Jack before she'd done something irretrievable.

She needed to immerse herself in work. Twenty-four seven.

'I'd like to take Dulcie out on Saturday for the morning, back to her place to see her animals. Are you happy to give her leave?'

Jack thought about it and then tilted his head in agreement. 'Of course. If you think she can manage it. It will be a good indication of her progress. I'll bring her out if you like.'

Eliza's hand tightened on the folder she carried and the paper actually creaked until she made herself loosen her grip. Jack at Dulcie's again was the last thing she wanted, but there was nothing she could do to stop him.

'If you think you should.' The words only just escaped her clenched teeth but he didn't notice. 'We'll finalise the time during the week.'

Jack seemed satisfied with that and finally he left the ward. Eliza walked away, turned into one of the empty rooms, leant back against the wall and closed her eyes. She was a fool, fool, fool!

Jack was confused and shaken by his response to Eliza last night and he was glad she wasn't making an issue out of a moment. The trouble was, he wasn't sure it had just been a moment. He didn't want to destroy something fragile by rushing something that they both weren't ready for. He'd done that with Lydia and had lived to regret it.

He certainly didn't want half the town, most of them relatives, breathing down his neck if he courted Eliza, but he wasn't certain Eliza understood that.

He hoped he hadn't hurt her. He'd apologise if he had the next time he saw her, but a part of him was relieved that, on the surface at least, she wasn't making a meal of last night. They'd sort it out. But he'd panicked when he'd pictured the buzz on the grapevine.

She didn't realise what this town was like, the power of the gossip, the accidental destruction that could happen. Though it seemed he'd done some destroying of his own.

He had full intentions of pursuing Eliza, if she'd have him after the way he'd put it so badly.

But he was beginning to realise that nothing was worth the price of losing Eliza.

During the rest of the week Jack found out just how elusive Eliza could be, but it only made him more determined to break down her reserve. He'd never had a hard time apologising to a woman before. Especially now that he accepted he was falling more in love with her every day.

Eliza's face kept him awake in the brief times he had to sleep or appeared in his mind when he opened his eyes in the morning. The memories of her skin against his, her breast beneath his hand and the connection he'd felt when he'd kissed her all taunted him.

As each day finished with Eliza more distant

than before, he began to hope the visit with Dulcie would clear the air because it would give them both some time away from work. It had better. He was beginning to feel obsessed with Eliza May and he didn't do obsession well.

On Friday night Eliza dusted and oiled furniture, although the smooth feel of the old timber made her think of Jack and the time she'd run her hands over his chest, solid and warm beneath her fingers. She had it bad. She scrubbed the kitchen, especially the table, but the memories wouldn't clear from the room.

She spread fresh flowers in vases around the little cottage and threw the sparkling windows wide because she could still imagine Jack beside her and she wanted the rooms fresh and untainted.

She wanted Dulcie to get as much joy out of her visit as possible—somebody should—and Eliza wanted to stay busy so she couldn't think of Jack back in this house again.

* * *

Saturday morning Eliza mowed the lawn and swept the verandas, and the activity almost kept her mind off the thought of Jack bringing Dulcie.

The weather turned on a sunny day and Eliza put extra chairs on the veranda in case Dulcie wanted to look out over the lawn.

She slipped into the shower an hour before they were due, and she dressed for Dulcie, not for Jack, but she needed to feel at her best for her self-esteem.

At ten o'clock Jack's car pulled up and Eliza met them at the gate.

Dulcie's eyes filled with tears. 'Eliza! It looks so wonderful.' Roxy barked and circled excitedly when she saw her mistress.

Jack, dressed in dark jeans and an open-necked shirt, looked so dear to her that Eliza's heart sank. It was too late. She did love him. How on earth was she going to get through this day?

He walked across with a white paper bag

balanced on his hand and a wicked smile on his face. 'I've brought a teacake.' He handed it ceremoniously to Eliza before he opened Dulcie's door and helped the older woman out of the car.

'Down, Roxy.' Dulcie laughed. 'Yes, I know you want to lick me. That's enough. Yucky.'

Eliza carried the cake and smiled at the dog's excitement, all the time feeling as though she were looking through thick glass at the scene. Jack looked across at her strangely a few times but she just stared blandly back.

When Roxy had calmed down, Jack followed Dulcie up the path to the veranda. Although the older woman managed the path without strain, the steps were not so easy.

'Take your time,' Eliza said quietly, and with Jack's help Dulcie finally reached her door.

Dulcie stared around with tears in her eyes. 'It all looks so wonderful. How can I ever thank you, Eliza?'

'You have—by letting me stay here.

Besides, your feather bed is much better than the Bellbrook Inn.'

She ushered Dulcie in. 'I bought biscuits because I'm a terrible cook, but now we have Jack's cake we'll put the kettle on and have a party.' She glanced at Dulcie's flushed face. 'How are you feeling?'

'I'm not doing too bad with my walking, but getting onto the veranda was more difficult than I'd bargained for.'

Jack stepped in. 'The occupational therapist will concentrate on steps this week and that should help. Don't rush—you're planning for the long term.'

'Sit down and I'll get the tea.' Eliza pulled out a firm chair from the table.

Dulcie smiled. 'Can I get it? I know I'm being impatient, but I'd like to see how I manage in the kitchen.'

Eliza winced at thought of being left with Jack. 'Fine, as long as Dr Jack carries the heavy teapot.'

Eliza and Jack stood in the centre of the room together and Eliza tried not to look into the kitchen where they had almost made love. When she glanced at him, Eliza found he was watching her.

'The cottage looks great, Eliza.' Those were his words but the expression in his eyes said, I remember you here.

Eliza felt the heat in her cheeks and looked away. She'd tried not to think about that day but obviously Jack had no such compunction.

She swallowed the lump in her throat and tried to keep her voice even. 'The cottage is easy to keep clean.'

Jack glanced towards the kitchen where Dulcie was still clattering dishes. 'I'd like to come back this evening. We need to talk, Eliza.'

Eliza shook her head vehemently. 'I'd prefer that you didn't!' She lowered her voice. 'There's nothing to talk about.'

Obviously Jack wasn't used to people

saying no to him. Well, he'd just have to learn, Eliza thought.

'You can't ignore what happened between us, Eliza.'

'I thought we both agreed nothing did happen. If it had, I could certainly ignore it.'

Dulcie's voice floated through. 'Can you carry the tray, Eliza, please?'

'I'll get it and come back for the pot,' Jack said, but he was watching Eliza as he stood up. Then he was gone but she could feel his look like a dose of sunburn.

This was too much. He'd discovered she was weak around him and he was relying on that weakness to break her resistance. What she couldn't figure was why he'd suddenly decided she was worth the effort.

Dulcie walked carefully back into the room and her face showed her obvious delight with her first kitchen enterprise. 'It wasn't too bad. To carry things is a problem, but I could buy myself a cake trolley until I get steadier.'

'Another couple of weeks will make a huge difference,' Jack said as he followed her with a large pink enamel teapot. 'Love the spout on this, Dulcie.'

'It was my mother-in-law's. She gave it to me before she died.'

Eliza tilted her head. 'I didn't know you were married.' Anything to take her mind away from Jack.

'Happily widowed,' she said, and Eliza had to smile.

'So who would be your next of kin? Do you have any children?' As soon as she said it Eliza remembered Jack had said Dulcie had a daughter she was estranged from. It was too late now to take the questions back.

Dulcie's eyes clouded. 'One—but we haven't seen each other for ten years. We're stubborn women, the Gardners, and it took my pregnancy before I made up with my own mother.'

'Maybe that's when I'll see mine, too,' Eliza said, and then wondered what had possessed her to blurt that out. She wasn't planning to get married, let alone the next step of having a baby, and she certainly had never thought of forgiving her mother enough to seek her out. Or maybe lately she had?

Many things seemed to be changing since she'd come to Bellbrook. She was more accepting of bushfires, was getting used to being the object of a town's conversation, could almost consider living in the country again, and now she was even contemplating finding her mother.

Dulcie reached across and patted Eliza's knee. 'And you've never heard from her in all that time?'

'She sends me birthday and Christmas cards but I've never answered.' It didn't actually sound very mature when she heard herself say it out loud. 'We haven't spoken since my father died.'

Dulcie shook her head. 'If she's still writing them she must be waiting for the day you answer.'

Jack lightened the moment. 'Well, if my mother were alive I would be speaking to her. But, then, men are much easier to get along with than women.'

'Yeah, right,' Eliza was glad to change the subject. 'Cut your cake and make a wish.'

Dulcie laughed and said, 'If you touch the plate with the knife, you have to kiss the nearest girl.'

Eliza felt a sense of *déjà vu*. Now, why on earth would she remember her mother had said that all those years ago? It was probably the only pleasant memory Eliza had of her, and she began to wonder if maybe she had only remembered the bad things.

'Oh, goody. I can rig this one.' Jack grinned and the devil glinted in his eyes as he raised the knife.

Eliza panicked. 'Well, that would be you, Dulcie. I'm off to wash up.' Eliza pushed back her chair but she wasn't quick enough.

Jack sliced into the cake, scraped noisily

against the plate underneath and swooped to drop a kiss on her cheek as she leant forward to rise. The kiss was warm and sweet and very quick, but Eliza felt the aftershocks of his lips on her skin and knew that she had to get out of there.

'And one for my other nearest girl.' Jack laughed and proceeded to peck Dulcie's cheek as well.

'Don't you hate a show-off?' Dulcie laughed but her cheeks were pink with pleasure.

The morning passed swiftly and before Dulcie began to tire they finished with a walk around the animals so Dulcie could say goodbye. Jack helped her back into his car.

'Thank you both so much. I've had a lovely morning.' Dulcie struggled with her seat belt but finally managed to do the clasp without help. 'I'll see you on Monday, Eliza.'

'You did beautifully, Dulcie.'

Jack walked round to the driver's side of his vehicle and paused before getting in. He looked at Eliza across the roof. 'I'll see you this evening.'

Eliza didn't flinch. She'd go out straight after she'd cleaned up. 'Not here, you won't.'

Before Eliza had a chance to get away, she heard the sound of Jack's car coming up the road and she gritted her teeth. He'd said evening. She dashed across, locked the front door and then scooted through to the kitchen to slip out the back.

Roxy appeared beside her but seemed torn between the sound of Jack's approaching car and walking with Eliza.

'Come with me.' Eliza urged the dog to follow her round the corner of the house and out into the shelter of the trees. If she stayed on the fence line, she should be protected from view. She stamped down the thought that she was being melodramatic.

'Eliza?' Jack's voice floated across the paddock and Roxy barked.

Eliza winced. 'For goodness' sake, Roxy. Either be quiet or go and see him, but don't come back to me.' Of course Roxy went to see Jack and showed him the way to Eliza.

Eliza resigned herself to looking foolish if she didn't find a good reason for lurking in the bushes and she glanced around frantically for one.

A vibrant patch of purple everlastings would have to do as a reason for her position. She began to break off the thick stems and had collected a sizable bunch before Jack appeared.

Jack tried not to smile at Eliza pretending to pick flowers. He'd seen her dash across the yard and had had a fair idea where she was even before Roxy had telegraphed to the world that her temporary mistress was hiding in the trees. 'Gone bush?'

Eliza tucked her hair behind her ear, but it promptly slipped out again. 'I asked you not to come.'

Asking was putting it kindly, Jack thought.

'Actually, it was more of an order not to visit.' Of course, that had made him want to come more.

She glared at him briefly and if she'd had any kind of fairy magic he would have keeled over from that look. Then she went back to picking those ugly flowers, which he couldn't see why anyone would want.

'You're not very good at following orders,' Eliza muttered.

He shrugged. 'Never have been—but I could learn.'

'I doubt it.' She wasn't meeting his eyes and that was frustrating in itself. This new wall she'd erected between them was currently impervious.

'What is it you want from me, Jack?' Now she was staring at him and the fire in her eyes made him wonder what he'd done to ignite this white rage. 'Are you looking for a free feed, a shoulder to cry on or just sex?'

He opened his mouth to dispute them all but she wouldn't let him talk.

'You don't want commitment, you've told me nothing about your past and you don't want your safe little world disturbed to risk your heart. Now you want a fling on the side as long as we keep it secret. What's in it for me, Jack?' She spread her arms wide and talked to the treetops. 'I'll tell you what's in it for me. Nothing.' She glared back at him. 'Now I'll tell you what I'm willing to risk! Also nothing! So there you go. We're the perfect pair to stay apart. Now, will you leave?'

'OK, Eliza. Maybe I haven't been fair to you at times but I'm trying now. I think we've been through too much together to act like we're strangers and pretend there's nothing between us.'

Eliza was implacable. 'There *is* nothing between us, Jack.'

'I'd like to take your word for that but I'm not so sure any more.'

Jack paused for a moment and looked around at the trees and the paddocks stretching away from this little woman who was growing so large in his life. He wasn't sure what he wanted but he knew they couldn't just be friends any more.

'You're being hard on me, Eliza. Without getting in too deep, you could let me show you the other side of me. Despite how I tried to bury it, there's more to me than being Bellbrook's only doctor.'

'Heaven forbid we get in too deep, Jack. I'm not sure there *is* more to Jack than the doctor.'

'Give me a chance. Come to my house.' He tilted his head and raised his eyebrows, like a kid asking for a treat.

'What if someone sees me, Jack? I thought you wanted to keep our non-relationship a secret?'

'I'm sorry I said that.' At least he now had the chance to say it. 'I have been sorry for a week but you've never let me near you. What we have, if it is a relationship or the beginning of one, is very young, and brittle, and easily damaged. I just didn't think you needed the well-intentioned interest of my many friends and relatives. I know I didn't.' He went on, persuasively, 'I'll make you dinner, so you can't say I just want a free feed. I've done my crying so I won't need your shoulder. And the sex is something we could discuss later.'

Her eyes widened in disbelief and he laughed. 'I was just baiting you. We don't have to discuss sex at all.'

They didn't need to discuss it. Just the mention of the word and the air became charged between them. Desire lay there between them like a big, soft, bouncy feather bed and both of them knew it. The searing memories had been there ever since that explosion of emotion and heat in Dulcie's tiny kitchen.

He hurried on. 'You could see my house. You must have wondered where and how I lived. What I do in my free time?'

'Never thought of it.' This time he knew

she'd lied because she looked away and then back at him with reluctance.

'Really?' He said mockingly. Caught you there, he thought, with the first glimmer of hope that this visit wouldn't be a complete failure.

Eliza tapped her knee for Roxy to come back to her and prepared to turn back to the house. 'You really do have tickets on yourself.'

She was running away and Jack couldn't let her. 'Well somebody has to vote for me when you obviously don't think I'm anything special.'

Eliza snorted. 'This whole town thinks the sun shines out of your…armpit. You don't need me to join them.'

She was waiting for the dog and then she was going to walk away from him. He needed to have the last word and get out of here with the upper hand. 'I'm not going to bicker with you, Eliza. You are invited to tea tomorrow night. I will expect you at eight.' He hoped she couldn't tell it was more bravado than expectation, but he had to try.

Eliza scoffed. 'Don't eat lunch as you might have two meals left over from your tea.'

She'd said 'might'. That was promising, he thought as he watched her walk away.

Sunday saw Eliza driving to Armidale with the top down and the wind blowing her troubles away. Except it didn't work. She'd hoped if she left the valley she'd get away from the memories of Jack.

Of course, she took him with her. Every bend in the road, every mountain she passed, every cloud in the sky made her think of the ups and downs of her relationship with Jack.

By the end of the day, when she turned back into Dulcie's driveway, she still didn't know what to do.

At seven-thirty Eliza stood indecisively in front of the mirror. So much had happened in the last few weeks, so many poignant events, emotion and heartache, and tonight could spell more drama. Should she give Jack one more chance to show promise for a future together or should she shield herself from the chance of more hurt?

The trouble was, the last thing she wanted to do was look back in years to come and regret not listening to him, just once.

If she went to dinner she wasn't committing herself to Jack for life. She doubted they could ever be just friends. It didn't feel like that. She felt finely balanced on the edge of something she wasn't sure she wanted and certainly didn't trust could be long-lasting. She wasn't quite back to the point of hoping something good could come of this.

The clock ticked and she wavered.

CHAPTER EIGHT

WHEN Jack opened the door, Eliza knew she was late but she was glad she'd taken the extra time to iron her favourite dress. It was emerald green and rustled when she walked, and she chose to wear it when she was feeling in need of extra strength. Eliza had never needed strength as much as she needed it tonight.

Jack's eyes widened appreciatively and he had a hidden smile, as if he'd found something especially pleasing.

'Come in, Eliza. You look beautiful and I'm so glad you came.' He showed her through the black-and-white-tiled entry into a book filled room that was a time warp of country life. Tapestry floral chairs, dark wood walls and rose-coloured carpets on the polished wooden floor all reflected from the huge wooden-framed mirror above the fireplace.

Jack's glance brushed over her again and she had no doubt of her welcome. 'I have a small present for you. I was going to give you this later but in view of your attire, I can't wait,' he said.

She'd never seen him like this—playful, at ease in his surroundings, the country gentleman.

He crossed to an old-fashioned dresser and lifted a cloth-wrapped pouch about the size of a small pineapple, which looked quite heavy. 'When I saw this, I knew I had to buy it for you.'

When she pulled the ribbon, the cloth fell away from a glass snowball sitting on top of a beautifully wrought wooden carving. The fairy inside the snowball was dressed in a billowing green frock very similar to Eliza's dress and she had bright green eyes, red hair and delicate silver wings.

Eliza laughed and shook the snow in the

ball. The fairy seemed to smile at her. 'Thank you. I've always loved these ornaments.'

'I'm glad.' He looked enormously pleased that she liked it. 'I think of you as the Queen of the Fairies.'

Eliza raised her eyebrows. 'And who are you?'

'Me?' He touched his chest. 'I'm hoping to be the handsome prince but something tells me you've picked me for an ogre.'

'Spare me. Please, not the martyr.' She looked away from him. 'So show me your home.'

Jack shrugged but there was pride in his glance around. 'As you can see, it hasn't changed much since my mother was alive. I'm not really into modern furniture and I have a fetish for polishing old wood. I find it soothing.'

He looked a little embarrassed at the admission and Eliza couldn't help teasing him.

'You make a very handsome housewife.' Eliza said, impressed despite herself. 'Are you sure you don't have a cleaning lady?'

He shook his head. 'Would you like to see

my ironing basket? Ironing doesn't turn me on at all.'

She knew what turned him on. My word, she did. Simple, irrelevant choice of words, but the connotations vibrated around the room so that Eliza could almost hear the clanging of danger signals.

They walked through to a glassed-in summer-room that overlooked the river and in the distance the Bellbrook Inn. An old-fashioned swing seat was positioned to capture the best of the rural view over the paddocks, the little sheds on the hills, dotted animals and the winding river.

This room was less formal but still bore the marks of an organised person. Eliza could tell this was his favourite part of the house. He gestured to the seat and she sat primly as far away from him as she could.

Conversation would be a good start, Eliza thought, shifting nervously. 'So, what do you do when you're not saving lives, Dr Dancer?'

'I play at farming but admit one of my cousins does the real farm maintenance. I like to fish, I eat my way around my relatives as a social butterfly, and I sit here and watch the world go by from the safety of my seat. Or I did before you came along.'

He began to swing gently and she wanted him to stop so she could concentrate on the situation. Why did men immediately have to start swinging as if they wanted to take off— couldn't they just ease into a slow glide? She dragged her feet to slow him down and he shot her a wicked glance and slowed to barely rocking.

'Going too fast for you, Eliza?'

'Hmm,' she said wryly, aware of his double meaning and not happy he could bait her so easily.

Eliza forced her shoulders to relax and looked out over the bluff at the view. She would prefer it if he didn't know just how nervous she felt, but couldn't hope he'd miss it. 'So this is how you saw Carla and I swimming that day.'

'And where I saw the fellow get stung the day before.'

She sniffed. 'So you say. I'm not sure that really happened.' She looked at him from under her brows. 'I think you just wanted to evict us from your river.'

'Nobody owns the river—or other people. You don't have to be afraid of me, Eliza.'

That was the problem, Eliza thought. She was the one with unrealistic yearnings. 'It's not you I'm afraid of.'

The silence lengthened as he caught her gaze and held it.

Then he smiled and it was the sweetest smile she'd ever seen. It tore a gentle hole in the fear around her heart like a feather through a spider web.

He leant across and touched her lips gently with his finger and then stood up. The spell broke and she blinked to reorientate herself.

How could a smile make her forget everything she'd promised herself? It was as if he'd kissed her!

'I'll just get the entrées and the champagne,' he said, as if nothing had happened.

Eliza fanned the heat in her face with her fingers but she didn't have as much time as she'd hoped to unscramble her brain.

A drinks trolley preceded him through the doorway. It was laden with tiny dishes of prawns and olives, and toothpicks with chicken and satay, and a big silver ice bucket with champagne and two glasses.

Eliza felt like an extra in the seduction scene. She didn't want to be the star. She tried to lighten the atmosphere. 'Your mother taught you well.'

'I like to have everything to hand. I hope you don't mind eating here instead of at the table?'

She shook her head. The view was incredible and Jack had brought napkins and side plates.

They sat on the swing and nibbled on juicy

prawns and tangy chicken and he encouraged her to at least sip the champagne.

But she still knew so little of his past.

'So tell me about the young Jack. What happened to your parents?'

He traced her shoulder with his fingertip and the sensation ran through her as he talked. She wasn't even sure he knew he was doing it. 'Mum and Dad died five years ago. They had a lot of trouble having kids—apparently it's genetic on my mother's side, but only passed down through daughters. She miscarried frequently and I can remember thinking that she should stop trying to have babies and just concentrate on me. She pretty well did except for those times when she was so incredibly sad at losing another child.

'Christmases with Mum started with church in the morning, presents when we came home and then she would cook and cook until the table would groan with the weight of turkeys and hams and rumballs and white Christmas cake and every vegetable, every fruit, punch bowls of fabulous non-alcoholic punch. We'd have ten or twenty for Christmas lunch, all relatives or friends so that Mum would feel there were enough people to share with.'

She squeezed his hand to hear more and he went on.

'My father was a simple man, incredibly intelligent but secure with his farm and his family and amazing with animals and their illnesses. When I grew older I realised he'd trained himself to be a vet just by reading books and connecting with the animals.

'When I was at uni I'd bring home my medical books and we'd sit and try to figure out something I couldn't understand. He'd read it once and be able to explain it to me so that I understood.

'I'd say to him that he could have been anything and he'd say what more could he want to be?'

'They sound amazing.' Eliza compared

Jack's wonderful home with her own and vowed her children would look back on their childhood like Jack could.

'I was very fortunate.'

Eliza squeezed his hand. 'What happened?'

'Dad was older than mum, he was eighty-two when he died. I found him leaning up against the bench in the work shed. He'd just slumped there and died when his heart gave out.'

'And your mother?'

Jack sighed. 'She'd had a lump in her breast that she'd told no one about, least of all her son, the doctor. Not long after Dad passed away she became sick and it was too late.'

'A year later I met my wife towards the end of uni and we married quickly, but that wasn't so good. I imagine Mary has told you what happened.'

Eliza nodded. 'One day you could tell me more but not now.'

He nodded. 'Mary is the sister I never had and Mick is my best friend.'

'Now there's you.' His voice was gentle as if he knew she considered flight. 'We connected from the first moment—didn't we, Eliza?'

She didn't answer for a moment because the simple question was loaded with extra weight—deep undercurrents that had appeared from nowhere. He didn't hurry her but she knew he was waiting for her answer.

She sighed. So this was it. Which way should she go? Keep fighting or let him in a little? But how would she stop? She couldn't lie. 'Yes, we did.'

'Was it the suddenness that shocked you, too?' he said quietly.

Eliza remembered her first sight of Jack and how she'd denied the chance of attraction so fiercely to herself. Eliza nodded but inside that huge bubble of fear and trepidation and disbelief was being melted by the warmth of his shoulder rubbing warmly against her and it felt so right. What she felt couldn't be a mistake.

Now the touch of even his shirtsleeve

seemed to have a life of its own by creating a field of energy between them.

Jack took her hand and drew it over into his lap and her fingers felt as if they glowed when he held them like that. She could see so many promises in his face but maybe that was just wishful thinking on her part. She felt incredibly aware of him as the silence lengthened and she had no control as the feeling built up.

This was all about touch and connection and without conscious thought her finger lifted and outlined his black brows and strong cheekbones.

He caught her fingers and kissed her palm, all the while not taking his eyes off her face, and she shuddered.

'This is what I am afraid of,' she said quietly. 'What if I let all this out and we connect like this and then you run away?'

'I would never do that—could never do that—once I gave you my heart.'

'Have you, Jack? Have you given me your heart?' Eliza ran her hand across his shoulder and down his arm. Just to touch him. In reassurance that he was really there and this was really happening.

'Yes.' His voice was very deep and she felt the goose-bumps rise on her arms.

It was too sudden. Too confusing. 'How long have you felt like this?' She needed to understand how this could happen.

He was watched her face as if willing her to believe him. 'It began on that first day. You had my heart as soon as you stared at me with those amazing eyes of yours. I thought you glowed like an angry fairy and when I looked into your eyes I couldn't breathe.'

Eliza shook her head. 'You were brusque.'

'I was in denial.'

She smiled. 'I know that feeling and I've been fighting it.'

'What about the way you responded to my kiss at Dulcie's?'

She blushed and he smiled at her confusion. 'That surprised us both, I think.'

'I don't know where that came from,' Eliza said.

His eyes darkened. 'Somewhere elemental, I should think. I've never experienced that loss of control before, like being sucked into a vortex.' His eyes caught hers. 'I think about that day a lot.'

She, calm and steady Eliza, was way out of her comfort zone. 'What are you doing to me, Jack? I can't believe how I'm feeling at the moment. It's too big to imagine you as the other half of me. How could we work together for these weeks and not have felt like this the whole time?'

He grimaced. 'We had walls up for protection, and past hurts, and other people needing us more than we could spare to give to ourselves.' He shrugged. 'Baggage. Fear our feelings wouldn't be returned.' He dragged her across so she was sitting in his lap, and the swing chair made protesting noises at the un-evenness of the weight.

They both laughed and the naturalness was such a wonder to Eliza she felt as if Jack had placed a spell on her—and she was supposed to be the magical one.

'Do you feel strange?' she asked him quietly.

He grinned back at her. 'Like Christmas morning as a kid, or waking up on your birthday, or your best friend has come to play and you've been waiting all morning and finally they are here and just as excited?'

'Yes.' Eliza thought about it. 'All of those.'

'Well, you should be excited because we have the most amazing future ahead of us.' Eliza fought down the fear that she couldn't quite let go of. It wouldn't be like before, he meant what he said, and the feel of him against her could only be honest.

It was the warmth that surrounded them that fascinated Eliza. Here with Jack she felt safe and relaxed and amazingly at home with a man half an hour ago she hadn't been sure she should even be visiting. How the heck had that happened?

So this was what it was like to really connect with someone.

She'd never felt anything like this towards either of the men she'd been going to marry. How frightening to think she could have settled for the wrong man and missed this total connection.

'Stop thinking!' Jack's voice intruded and she turned to face him. 'Don't think of anything but us at this moment because people wait their whole lives for a minute of this feeling—let's dissect it later.'

Eliza nodded and she put her hands around his neck and stared into his eyes. 'You're right. Sometimes I think too much. Sitting here feels wonderful.'

'It's going to get better.'

'Show-off.'

When Jack kissed Eliza for only the second

time it was a homecoming. His lips on hers, the gentle fan of his breath on her face and the rub of his cheek against hers created more magic. When he pulled away to smile and then kiss her again, she laughed with the joy of it. The wonder of his hands cradling her face as he tried to convey how much he treasured her was the moment that splintered the last of the ice around Eliza's heart and she felt the tears sting her eyes.

'I'm terrified. What if something happens to take this away? I've waited my whole life to believe in love.'

'Shh. Let me kiss you.'

They kissed until the sun went down and then he took her hand and drew her into his bedroom, austere and practical with dark heavy furniture, but Eliza didn't notice.

The green dress fell to the floor, along with his shirt and trousers, and soon they were naked. He took her hand and led her to the old-fashioned bed where she lay like a pagan princess as he turned away briefly to protect her from pregnancy.

In a way she was glad of this moment to breathe and ground herself in what had become such a storm of emotion. A tiny flicker of doubt almost broke through but then Jack was back and they touched with heated skin on heated skin. They lay still for a moment just feeling the velvet between them until Jack raised one hand and stroked her breast.

'So beautiful. So lush and yet you are so tiny. I'm afraid I'll break you.'

Eliza ran her hand over the solid curves of his chest, 'Gorgeous,' she said. 'I'm not afraid at all.' And kissed his throat.

Then they meshed, sliding, hands caressing and mouths seeking. A wondrous blur of sensations with joy and discovery that had no place in time. No haste, but not too slowly, until Eliza cried out and Jack hugged her close with his own damp eyes.

She'd never dreamed it could be like this, so

much a moment of togetherness and bonding. She lay snuggled in his arms and accepted that with Jack she'd found her place.

Before dawn, Eliza slipped out of bed and showered. Jack made her a coffee and then kissed her again, and the next time she looked at the clock she knew that by the time she'd driven home, fed the animals and dressed for work, she would be late.

'I have to go now, Jack. I'll be late.'

'I know,' he said, grinning, and then his phone rang. It was a callout and he'd have to go as well.

Eliza drove home and the dawn had never seemed so beautiful.

Eliza was in the shower when the phone rang.

'Eliza? It's Mary. My waters have broken, the ambulance is up in the bush somewhere with Jack and Mick, and the pains are coming every three minutes. I don't think I can drive.'

'You'll be fine, Mary. Have your bag ready

and…' she did a quick calculation of the five minutes into town and then the ten out to Mary's '…I'll be there in about fifteen minutes.' That only left her time to throw on a pair of trousers, a T-shirt and her running shoes.

When Eliza pulled up in a cloud of gravel in front of the McGuinnesses place the lights were still on all over the house and Mary was waiting on a chair beside the door.

She didn't get up when Eliza climbed out of her car and by the time she'd made it to her side, Eliza could see she was in strong labour.

'Well, I guess you'll have your baby at Bellbrook. Seems only natural.'

Mary tried to smile but beads of sweat stood out on her forehead. 'I honestly thought I would have time to get to Armidale.'

'Let's concentrate on getting you somewhere achievable, like my car. I'll even let you sit on my white seats.'

Mary swallowed a bubble of hysterical laughter and took a deep breath. 'I don't know if I can walk.'

Eliza hadn't worked in labour wards for nothing. 'Of course you can walk! Up you get.' She slid her hand under Mary's armpit and heaved her out of the seat.

'You're quite strong for a little woman, aren't you?' Mary gasped, and Eliza chuckled.

'You have no idea.'

They made it to the car before the next pain, and Mary smiled weakly when she saw that Eliza had covered her seats with a pile of towels. 'Hopefully I won't soak through those.'

Eliza shut the door on her and sprinted round to the driver's side. 'Least of my worries at the moment. Let's get you into town.'

Eliza passed Mary her mobile phone. 'Get Rhonda to prepare for the birth and to try and get a message through to Mick and Jack. I'd really like those two to be here for you when the time comes.'

'Me, too, but I don't like their chances.' Mary moaned.

Eliza shot her a look as she accelerated around a corner. 'Hang on, Mary. It's much nicer if you can do this near a bed.'

They arrived at the hospital with a squeal of brakes and Rhonda was at the door with a wheelchair. It took three of them to get Mary out of the car and about sixty seconds to get her into a spare room that Rhonda had set up as an emergency labour room.

Eliza was privately glad they weren't going back into the emergency room they'd had the drama in earlier.

'Thanks, Rhonda,' she said, and Rhonda nodded. Eliza had another thought. 'Do we keep Syntocinon or Pitocin here for after birth?'

'It's drawn up and on the bedside cabinet.'

'You're an angel because we're going to need it soon.'

To Mary she said, 'Let's get you into a gown and onto the bed, Mary. I'd love to have a feel of your tummy and a listen to your baby's heart rate, if that's OK.'

As soon as Mary was settled, Eliza quickly palpated Mary's large belly and established that baby was lying head first, and on his mother's right side. Then she used the old-fashioned trumpet-shaped foetal stethoscope, one end of the metal tube resting against Mary's tummy and the other against Eliza's ear. She glanced at her watch and counted the galloping heart rate that trembled in her ear.

'One hundred and fifty. Perfectly normal despite the fact that someone pulled the plug out of his or her bath and they're sliding towards the exit sign.'

'Only a midwife would say that,' Mary gasped, as the next pain surged over her. 'I feel like pushing.'

Murphy's law, Eliza thought, and prepared for the birth.

Out loud she said, 'That's fine, Mary. Just

listen to your body and do what it tells you to do.'

'It's telling me to push.' Mary sucked the air into her lungs and proceeded to do just that.

'Well I didn't have to worry about getting your dilatation wrong because I can see a little patch of brown hair—your cervix is certainly out of the way.'

Another screech of brakes outside heralded the arrival of Mick and Jack, and the door burst open to admit the dishevelled men.

Mick was wild-eyed and black with soot from head to foot. 'Oh, my God, Mary, my love, I'm so sorry I wasn't here for you.'

Mary just grasped her husband's hand and pushed again.

Jack took one look at the progress Mary had made already and rushed to the basin to wash his black hands.

He spoke over his shoulder to Eliza. 'Have you got oxytocics for after the birth?'

'Yes. Rhonda has it all prepared. If you're

not ready soon, I'll have to catch this nephew or niece of yours so get your gloves on, Dr Dancer.'

Jack grinned at Eliza and briefly a flash of warmth flared between them before he pulled his gloves on hurriedly. Once he was gloved, Eliza stepped back and picked up the camera from Mary's bag.

Within two minutes Mary and Mick's new daughter was lying on her mother's stomach gazing up at her mother like a possum. Eliza took a quick series of photos and everybody sighed with relief, although Eliza wasn't happy with the new baby's colour. She shifted the tiny oxygen tubing nearer the newborn's face.

Mary stretched down and kissed her daughter on the forehead. 'I want to call her Amelia.'

'She looks blue.' Mick's voice was strangled by the overload of emotion from the last few minutes.

She did. Eliza placed her hand on his arm. 'So would you if you'd come through the tunnel that fast. Give her a couple of seconds to catch her breath and we'll check her out.'

Eliza glanced at Jack as she reconnected the oxygen bag and mask onto the tubing and gave a few clearing inflations as she held it over Amelia's face. The baby girl was still pale and although blue-tinged hands and feet were normal with newborns, Amelia's tummy was as blue as her lips. Her central cyanosis was deepening.

Jack was distracted by extra bleeding that suddenly gushed at the business end of the bed with the imminent delivery of the placenta, and Eliza prayed that Amelia would be fine. She'd seen something similar a few years previously and that ending hadn't been good. Amelia didn't look fine.

'I need you up here, Jack,' she said quietly, and her words sliced into his concentration. He blinked and focussed on the baby. 'I think you should listen to her heart,' Eliza said.

CHAPTER NINE

MICK looked from Eliza to Jack and then at his daughter. Even as a layman he could tell something was deeply wrong.

He went to speak but Mary laid her hand on his arm and gripped him. 'Wait,' she said, and there was a deep resignation in her voice that frightened him more.

'What's going on?' His voice had risen and Mary squeezed his arm sharply.

'They don't know! Give them time to find out, love.'

He subsided but the tears formed in his eyes as he looked at his daughter. She was deeply blue and her respiration rate had risen despite the oxygen that Eliza held to her face. Now

Eliza was assisting the respirations with squeezes of the bag, but Amelia's blueness continued to deepen.

'Her heart sounds are all over the place. Apart from the patent ductus, she has back-flow into every chamber. Probably stiff lungs as well, as the ventilations aren't working well.'

Urgently Eliza assisted Jack to insert an endotracheal tube—to ensure the most efficient oxygenation to Amelia—but it didn't help.

'Get MIRA on the phone.' Jack shot the order at Eliza, and she nodded and sped over to the emergency phone number list and grabbed the hand phone.

'My poor baby,' Mary said, and her eyes filled with tears. Mick looked from Jack, to Mary, and then to Eliza—as if one of them at least would give him hope. All the faces said the same and it was unthinkable.

'What's that? What's going on? Do something, Jack,' Mick cried.

'MIRA is the mobile infant retrieval team in

Sydney, Mick, to see if there is anything else we can do.' He kept his eyes on the new father—Mary knew all this too well.

'They are our only hope. I think Amelia has serious congenital heart and lung problems that make it incredibly hard for her to live outside the uterus. Inside the uterus, she was fine while Mary was supplying the oxygenated blood via the placenta. The blood didn't need to go through the parts of Amelia's heart and lungs that aren't functioning. Now she has been born she can't get enough oxygen to her brain and other organs because her heart and lungs aren't working anywhere near properly.'

Eliza handed the phone to Jack. 'It's Dr Hunter Morgan from MIRA, Jack.'

Jack closed his eyes for a second to clear his brain and then spoke into the phone to explain Amelia's problem.

All they could do was listen to Jack's end of the conversation. 'We've done that. And that. Yes. No. No improvement. All of that, too.' He looked at them all and the pain in his eyes was mirrored in theirs.

Jack's voice had risen slightly. 'Isn't there any thing else we can try?' There was a long pause. Jack's voice dropped and the final words were a whisper. 'I see. Thank you,' Jack said. 'We may as well take it out, then.' Jack looked at Eliza and mimed removing the ET tube.

'Goodbye.' He put the phone down.

Eliza closed her eyes and then opened them to do what was asked. It was the little things like this that broke you up. Amelia's little face returned to normality without the plastic tube distorting her features. It was good the tube was gone for her last few minutes.

Mary nodded and she bit her lip so hard a drop of blood appeared at the corner. She gathered her daughter closer to her heart and held on for dear life. Her daughter's life.

Jack turned to the parents. 'I'm sorry, Mick, Mary. There's nothing I can do.'

Mick shook his head. 'You're sorry? What do

you mean, you're sorry? Get a chopper. Get them to fly her somewhere she can get help.'

Mary stroked her husband's arm. 'It's too late, darling. Even the best hospital in the world couldn't save her. She stayed alive to meet us but now she has to go.'

Mick looked at his wife as if she were mad. 'Go? Go where? You can't just let her die.'

Rhonda fled from the room. Jack watched her go and wished he could go, too. He couldn't take any more from this day. This was too horrific—but Mary and Mick needed him. He looked across at Eliza and thanked God she was here to at least share the burden.

She looked quite composed, in fact. He found that irked him. Of course she was composed. She'd even looked composed when she'd woken in his arms that morning. We're all just ships in the night for her. But this was tearing his guts out and Mary was looking at him as if he'd tell her she was wrong and her daughter would be alive this time tomorrow.

'Amelia's going to die, Mary,' he said in a strangled voice, and before he knew it he was kneeling beside the bed and weeping as if his heart were broken. Weeping for Mary and Mick and Amelia, and for himself and baby he lost three years ago. The three of them formed a hand-holding circle around Mary's baby as she turned darker and darker and her breaths turned to gasps.

Eliza looked on, excluded by their closeness and crying inside for all of them. But someone had to steer the ship and she quietly went about the business of preparing for the worst.

She cleared the room of the debris from the birth, gathered fresh clothes for Mary and made tea and coffee for Jack and Mick.

Eliza was the one who dressed Amelia in beautiful clothes so she could lie with her mother. She gently suggested Mary have more photos and handprints taken to treasure in the future, which she then proceeded to take.

She arranged for the minister to come and

baptise Amelia and talk with the parents and greet the relatives that began to trickle in with the news. And the sun brought the heat of a new day.

Mary and Mick were lying together on the bed with their hands around their cooling baby daughter, and Jack left the room like a zombie and shuffled his way to his car.

He couldn't believe this had just happened. What should have been a joyous event was a tragedy he didn't feel he would ever get over. Good people like Mary and Mick shouldn't have to endure this. Nobody should have to endure this loss.

The events of this morning brought back all of the pain of losing his wife and son, and the combination had meant he'd lost it in there. He'd promised himself three years ago he wouldn't cry. In front of everyone! In front of Eliza who had been the professional one!

'You can't drive home, Jack.' Eliza spoke

quietly beside him and he turned towards her with stricken eyes. He tried to speak but couldn't and Eliza moved to wrap her arms around him, but he stepped back.

Eliza felt as though he'd slapped her. 'I know you are devastated, Jack. We all are.'

Finally he found the words and all the anger at the repeated unfairness of fate spilled from his lips in a torrent of grief aimed directly at Eliza. 'You don't know anything. You were as cool as a cucumber in there. You're all on the surface, Eliza. You're like Lydia, no depth. I can see that now. Stay away from me.'

Eliza felt the air whoosh from her lungs as if she'd been stabbed in the solar plexus. 'You don't mean that, Jack. I care for Mary a lot…and I care for you.'

'You care for Eliza, full stop. You can handle anything—so handle this. I'm not coming in today and maybe not tomorrow either, and I'm taking the weekend off as well.' And with that he wrenched open his car door and climbed awkwardly into the seat. He didn't look back and Eliza watched in disbelief and horror as he drove away from her with his harsh words indelibly printed in her brain.

Eliza wanted to run. And hide. Hide like her father had and like she always did from situations that were too painful.

Jack had the power to hurt her because she'd fallen in love with the wrong man—again. Only this time it was a hundred times worse than before.

If Jack thought she was unaffected by Amelia's death then he hadn't ever really seen her. He was just another man who had leant on her and not been interested in the real Eliza.

Eliza's neck drooped as the weight of Jack's outburst hung over her. She lifted her eyes and stared at the glint of sunlight that was his car in the distance.

Jack was wrong about her, but that was his

problem. And she couldn't run. Normally, working for the agency allowed her to leave but this time she wouldn't go. Mary needed her and the hurtful, harmful things Jack had said didn't change that.

He might think they were true, and the old Eliza might have thought she had been rejected again because she was worthless, but this time she'd stay as long as Mary needed her.

Jack might look at her with horror and say she didn't cry, but inside she'd been weeping rivers of tears for two beautiful people and their baby daughter who'd had the shortest time together. But they had had time together—Amelia had waited to meet her parents before she'd left, and Mary and Mick would learn to treasure those few owlish looks from their daughter before she'd closed her eyes for ever.

Eliza turned and entered the hospital. Rhonda would finish her shift in an hour and Eliza had just enough time to go home, shower and feed the animals before she needed to come back for the day.

On the drive home she passed the spot where the unknown woman had driven off the edge of the ravine, and she wondered how they both were. How tragically ironic that those two had survived such a horrific accident and yet Mary's baby had died from a natural birth. Eliza wondered what God's grand plan had in store for that other baby girl.

It must be something amazing to spare her against such odds. And what special mission had Amelia accomplished during her few minutes of life?

Now the tears started to fall and Eliza pulled in under the moon gate and parked her car in front of Dulcie's house. Her head fell down on the edge of the steering-wheel and great racking sobs tore from her chest and she sobbed as if she would never stop.

After a few minutes she raised her head and realised that Roxy was howling outside the car door. Eliza drew a deep breath and turned the handle to let her in. The dog stood up on her hind legs and buried her wet nose under Eliza's armpit.

'Yes, you can lick me,' Eliza said, and then she climbed out of the car and hugged the warm body of the dog. She stood up and the sun shone in her eyes and Poco the donkey brayed for attention.

One of the roosters crowed and Eliza headed for the pens. She may as well do all this in these clothes, at least it would be easier to climb the fence with her trousers on.

By seven a.m. Eliza was back at the hospital and a shattered Rhonda went home.

Eliza carried the breakfast tray into Mary's room and to her surprise she found Mick was gone.

Mary looked up, saw Eliza and held open her arms.

'Thank you for everything, you wonderful,

wonderful woman,' she said in a broken voice. Eliza almost dropped the tray in her hurry to return the hug.

'I'm so sorry, Mary. Amelia is so perfect and beautiful but here so short a time. We're all devastated.'

'I know. I thank God every minute that she was born here, with my friends around me, and not somewhere cold and distant where I didn't know the staff and where they might have whisked her away to die away from me. I'm just sorry you had to carry the burden on your own, Eliza. I know you have.

'Poor Jack is distraught—it must be like losing my sister and his son all over again. But maybe part of Amelia's gift will be the healing of Jack now that he has allowed himself to grieve for his own child along with mine.'

She shrugged painfully and closed her eyes as the grief overwhelmed her again.

Eliza couldn't believe that Mary could still think of others through her own pain. She wasn't sure that Jack was worth it, the way he'd just treated her. She brushed her own tears away and raised her chin. 'Where's Mick?'

'He's gone home to shower and have breakfast. He's angry at fate and he's angry at me because he says I was too accepting, but that's a man's way. They hit out when they see our strength because they know they are nowhere near as strong. Strong women frighten them.'

Eliza saw the wisdom in Mary's quiet words and it was as if a light shone brightly out of the darkness. Now was not the time to sort this out, but later things would change. That concept would explain so many things in her life.

'You are right, Mary,' she said resolutely, and there was something in Eliza's voice that made Mary look at her. Strength passed between them and then they both looked at the tiny cot in the corner. Without a word Eliza brought Mary's daughter to her for a kiss.

'I'll go home this afternoon,' Mary said. 'The visitors can come here instead of home and before dark we'll say goodbye to Amelia and leave her with you.'

Eliza nodded and the day started.

Mary showered and pushed her breakfast around her plate, and all the time Amelia stayed in the room with her mother.

'These are sad days for the hospital, Eliza. First that terrible accident and now Matron's baby.' Dulcie Gardner's blue eyes were even paler with tears.

'Yes, Dulcie. But comfort is found in strange places. Like me minding your house for you. I went home so upset this morning I cried, and do you know who gave me comfort? Your dog, Roxy. She was so wonderful and I realised how lucky I was to be in that place at that time.'

'I'm glad, my dear.' And indeed she did look brighter to think that her dog had helped.

'How do I stop her licking me, though?' Eliza asked as she helped Dulcie put on her shoes.

Dulcie nodded. 'She does have a busy tongue. Just say, "Yucky," and she'll step back.'

When they both smiled, they stopped and looked at each other, and Eliza thought of the strength of women. A man would think they were callous but they were carrying the pain of loss yet moving on.

'Did they ever find out who that poor young woman was?' Dulcie asked.

'Not yet. Or who she was visiting. She's not off the critical list, yet but the baby is doing well.' Eliza finished tidying the room.

Eliza heard Dulcie talking to herself as she left. 'That's a blessing, then. Poor little mite.'

True to his word Jack didn't come in, even to see Mary before she left, though he phoned her.

Donna came in for the night shift an hour early and shooed Eliza home.

'You've done a mammoth job, and everyone knows it. The hospital thanks you, Eliza.'

'Donna! Thank you. Rhonda was wonderful, too. And thank you for coming in early. I must admit I'm shattered and will be glad when

Friday comes and I can have days off. This has been the week from hell.'

Donna nodded vehement agreement. 'Jack's feeling it too. I've never known him to take more than a day off before.'

Eliza did not want to talk about Jack. 'More fool him, then. Goodnight, Donna.'

At home, Eliza watered the animals and then wandered down to the creek, where the steady trickle of water splashed over pink and yellow pebbles in the creek bed.

No other sounds intruded except birds, cracking twigs from Roxy hunting in the undergrowth and the evening wind in the tops of the trees. The sun was still red-ringed with smoke. It hung low in the sky, but the heat from the day was still in the air. There was a deeper swimming hole at a bend in the creek where if she stripped off her clothes she'd be able to sit or lie in the water and get cool.

Eliza glanced around and, of course, there

was no one in sight. She shrugged out of her clothes. Soon she was lying on her elbows with the cold water swirling around her, draining the tension from her body and washing away the hurtful things that Jack had said.

Mary's words came back to her and Eliza wondered if she truly had such strength, maybe that was why men in her past had come for healing and then left. It made sense.

Perhaps even her mother leaving her father, because she had been strong enough to do so, made sense. And her own father, leaning on her, retreating from society because he didn't need them while he had Eliza, using her strength because he couldn't go on without it. She felt the weight of failure she'd carried with her drifting away down the creek.

Her mother leaving hadn't been Eliza's fault. The fact that her mother had been able to walk away from her daughter showed enormous strength, and maybe one day Eliza would find her and ask why.

Eliza stood up from the water and waded back to the bank. She might be strong but she was bone tired and needed to sleep.

The next morning Eliza took an apple down to the gate and Poco obligingly moved away. She'd been too tired to remember that yesterday. Eliza grinned at the grey-nosed donkey. 'I've got your secret now, haven't I, old son?'

On the drive into the hospital the day promised to be a little cooler. In fact, Eliza wondered if there were rainclouds gathering on the horizon again.

Considering the past week, the day was uneventful and again Jack didn't show up. Eliza had a few minor outpatients, which she managed on her own, and anyone she was worried about she consulted Armidale's outpatient clinic before sending them home.

After work she drove out to Mary and Mick's house and spent half an hour with them. She left a cooked chicken and bread rolls from the shop in case Mary didn't feel like cooking, but refused Mary's offer to join them. She judged them best visited in short bursts.

The rest of the week followed the same pattern and Eliza didn't try to vary it. She was too thankful for the brief window of relief from Jack.

On Friday night, Eliza arrived home and it was still light. What should she do? It seemed like for ever since she'd had two days off work and she didn't know how to fill the time.

She could go to see Jack but more than likely such a visit would open her up for more pain.

A visit to Jack might help him, not herself, and it was time she nurtured herself without saving others.

She deserved it.

She was worth it.

'I'm worth it.' It felt good just to say that out loud.

She would stay home with the animals and

potter. She would lie in the sun with a book and doze in the afternoon and renew her spirit. Her soul needed it and from now on she would look after herself.

Eliza waited for Jack to do his morning round on Monday and she remembered the first day she'd waited for him.

It felt so long ago. Since then she'd seen so many sides of him.

He had a caring side with all his patients, like Dulcie, waiting with the sick woman and worrying about her pets.

She'd seen the strong and efficient side, with the unknown woman and her emergency Caesarean. Not many doctors would have handled that situation so calmly.

Then there was his humorous side, his puns and sense of the ridiculous that could make her laugh.

But his tortured side was too deep. too hurtful, and he made her cry. She didn't need that.

Regardless of how much her emotions were involved, she wasn't going to sacrifice herself on the altar of Jack's needs.

The tiny flicker of hope that had whispered he might someday come to her as a whole man was gone. It had disappeared into the sunrise with his car last Monday.

Now she could hear his voice rise to greet someone outside and then his footsteps echoed down the corridor. Eliza waited at the nurses' station with a neutral expression on her face.

Jack had no idea where the last week had gone. He'd been to see Mary and Mick at least once each day but otherwise his phone hadn't rung and he hadn't left his house.

It was time to put all the grief behind him and move on—which meant he had to return to work!

And face Eliza.

This would be the hardest part.

He knew that he'd been unfair to her. And

not just because he'd left the whole responsibility of the hospital with her. He'd been cruel and unjustified in his lashing out. Although he couldn't remember exactly what he'd said on the morning of Amelia's birth, he knew he'd dumped his grief and pain and uselessness on the one person he shouldn't have. Why were people always hardest on the ones they loved?

The incredible night he'd spent with Eliza in his arms felt like a distant dream, and he'd failed her when he'd known how fragile she was with giving her heart. He just hoped she'd forgive him.

Jack rounded the corner. There she was! Five feet nothing and terrifyingly efficient. In fact—plain terrifying. She made him feel things he'd vowed never to feel again and unlike Lydia she didn't need him to look after her. He probably had nothing to offer her that she couldn't get for herself. If she ever forgave him.

Her hair swung around her cheekbones as

she glanced away and then back at him, and he couldn't tell if she was still angry because she didn't meet his eyes.

CHAPTER TEN

'HELLO, Eliza,' Jack said.

Jack looked older and drawn, and Eliza fought the impulse to pull his head down on her chest and tell him it would be all right.

He didn't want her and even if he did, he'd be another millstone around her neck because he couldn't free himself from his past. He'd have to wake up to himself without her.

She'd been there. Loving emotionally scarred men who couldn't return unconditional love, and the cost was too high. She wasn't going back.

'Good morning, Doctor.' She didn't give him time to comment on her formality. 'Dulcie is coming along well. She managed to dress herself completely this morning, though we still need to work on her step-climbing.'

'Excellent. How are you coping with the animals?'

'Fine.' She picked up her pace and smiled at her patient as she rounded the corner into Dulcie's room. Jack could do nothing but follow.

'Matron tells me you are improving every day, Dulcie,' he said.

'I think so. What I want to know is how well am I going to get, Dr Jack? I'm eager to get home and I did well on my first visit. I'm too young for this invalid stuff.'

Jack nodded in sympathy. 'I'll speak to the occupational therapist today and see if there are any improvements we could make in your house to make it safer. I know she thinks you're progressing well.'

Dulcie had questions that she'd had time to think about. 'Am I at risk of having another stroke or will the blood-thinning medication I'm on now stop that?'

'The tablets you're on will certainly cut down the risk, and in a way you were lucky to have a mild stroke and warn us that you were in danger of a major stroke, which would be a lot harder to recover from.'

Jack hesitated. 'I'm hoping you'll return to almost full strength in your right side within the next month and you should be home in less than a week if we get everything right.'

Dulcie smiled with relief. 'I can wait if the news is going to be that good. For a while there I thought I was gone. There are a few things I need to straighten up before I die.'

'Well I'm hoping you'll live a long and productive life, Dulcie, so don't talk about dying yet.'

They left Dulcie and did a quick check with the seniors and all the time Jack tried to start a personal conversation. Eliza was having none of it.

'Well that's it, thank you, Doctor. Have a good day.' Eliza spun on her heel and walked back towards Dulcie. She could feel his eyes on her as she went, but it was better this way.

'Eliza. Stop!'

His voice was quiet but there was a note of command in it she'd never heard before. Despite herself, Eliza stopped.

'Please, look at me.'

She stared at the corridor in front of her for a moment and then her shoulders stiffened as she turned. She would not allow him to hurt her again.

'Yes?'

He took three steps and then he was right beside her and she could feel the heat coming from his body because he was close. Too close.

'I need to apologise for the things I said after Amelia died.' He looked down into her face and his dark eyes were shadowed with remembered grief.

He was still thinking about himself, not her— or them. *He needed* to apologise for his own sake, not for hers or for what they had between them. 'If that's what you need to do, then go ahead.'

He winced and Eliza sighed. It would be better to get this over quickly instead of being confrontational. 'Forget I said that. I'm listening.'

He stared at her for a moment as if to judge how receptive she was, and then gave a tiny shrug.

'I was overwrought and to attack you was unforgivable. In my defence, the last few days had been especially emotional—not just with the present but with a lot of issues I should have dealt with years ago. You have helped me with those too, Eliza, and I had no right to take my pain out on you. I am deeply sorry.' He even looked the part. As apologies went, it was fairly impressive.

Eliza could feel the tears prickling behind her eyes but she had too much at stake herself!

'All right, Jack. I know what sort of week

you'd had—because I had it, too. You hurt me but you woke me up as well. The big discovery is I *am* passing through here and we'd both do well to remember that.'

Jack shook his head in denial. 'There is more than that between us, but I guess we can start there.' He held out his hand. 'Friends?'

Eliza shook her head. 'No. I'm not interested. There is no start to any relationship between us. Julie is looking for my replacement now.'

That night Jack tried to speak to Eliza at her house but she refused to open the door. She turned off the outside light and turned the television up so he couldn't even talk to her through the wood.

On Tuesday he called again and left a teacake and flowers on her step.

When he called around on Wednesday night the flowers were dry and wilted and a dog dish sat where he'd rested the cake.

* * *

On Thursday morning news came through that the police had identified the young woman from the crash. Two policemen from Armidale appeared at the hospital and asked for Dulcie Gardner.

Eliza tried to contact Jack but he was on a call and out of range. She could only hold Dulcie's hand as the news was broken to her and they both sat, stunned. The driver had been identified as Bronte Gardner, Dulcie's daughter, and she was still in serious condition in a Sydney hospital.

When the policemen left, Dulcie looked up at Eliza, pain and confusion and guilt dark in her eyes.

Her voice cracked. 'How could I not know my daughter was fighting for her life?' She clutched at Eliza's hand. 'Go and see your mother, Eliza, before you end up with regrets it will be too late to do anything about.'

Eliza nodded, because it was the only

comfort she could give. 'We'll arrange for you to see Bronte as soon as possible, Dulcie.'

'I know.' She bit her lip. 'I feel so helpless and useless. I think I'd like to be by myself. I know I can call you if I need you.'

Eliza hugged her and slipped out of the room and closed the door.

Eliza leaned back against the corridor wall and closed her eyes. She saw the woman she now knew as Bronte Gardner in her memory, and the events that had followed were something she would never forget. Perhaps Bronte and her baby would come back here for a while to spend time with Dulcie.

It was almost too much to grasp. When Eliza opened her eyes, Jack was there.

Jack had picked up Eliza's missed call on his mobile, and had called in at the hospital on his way back to the surgery. He suspected there would be no light reason for Eliza to call him after the way she'd been with him all week, but he hadn't expected her to look as lost and vulnerable as she'd looked, leaning against the wall with her eyes closed.

His step quickened and he moved up beside her. 'Eliza? Are you all right?'

'No. I don't think I am.' It was a moment of weakness he didn't expect as she stepped forward and leant her head on his chest. Automatically Jack put his arms around her. She was soft and forlorn against him and he tilted her chin up with his finger and searched her face. Her eyes were huge damp pools of green and he felt that jolt he'd suffered the first day he'd seen her. He searched for something to keep himself from crushing her to him.

'Since when do you admit to human frailty?'

She buried her chin into his chest again and mumbled into his shirt. 'The woman from the car is Dulcie's daughter.'

Jack nodded his head. 'Ah. Poor Dulcie. I was afraid she would be. After we talked the other day I passed my suspicions on to the police and they were going to follow it up.' He felt Eliza stiffen beneath his hand as she stepped back. He seemed to have found another way to alienate her.

She lifted her chin and sniffed. 'Of course, you didn't think to warn me?' Those damn eyes had changed again and he deeply regretted she'd pushed him away because the possibilities had been good. He was beginning to feel that the only way he was going to pierce Eliza's shell was to get her into his arms and kiss her.

'It was only a suspicion and I hoped my hunch was wrong.' He glanced towards Dulcie's closed door. 'How is she?'

'Devastated and guilty she didn't try harder to contact her daughter in the past. You go in and see her. I'll make her a cup of tea. Would you like one?' He shook his head and she watched him knock and enter the room.

When Jack left, Eliza went back in to Dulcie. The older woman's eyes were red-rimmed and Eliza sat on the arm of her chair and put her arm around her shoulder.

'I'm so lucky it's not too late to say all the things I should have said. She was a lovely little girl, you know—but we clashed so badly when she became a teenager, and I was young, too. My husband used to say we were too much alike.'

Eliza didn't say anything. She just listened.

Dulcie stared out the window as if she could see all the way to Sydney. 'Dr Jack says there doesn't seem to be a father in the wings, so the baby is being looked after by the hospital until Bronte is well enough to look after her. Dr Jack is going to ring her doctors and find out what he can for me. She will get better, won't she?'

Eliza nodded. 'The hospital she's in is a major centre with a wonderful reputation. I'm sure she will. She must be a fighter to have done so well.'

Dulcie looked up at Eliza and her voice was stronger. 'I could help. I've been given another chance to right the wrongs with my daughter. I just hope she'll come to me when she can. It seems she'd already decided to come once, hopefully she will again.'

'I'm sure she will, and I know you will be a wonderful mother and grandmother.'

Dulcie shook her head in distress. 'How will I manage? When should I try to manage? I want to do the right thing.'

Eliza squeezed her hand. 'Take things slowly and we'll arrange help when they arrive and until you all get settled. You could even have a day or two here to get used to each other and caring for the baby. You're still young, Dulcie. You'll be fine.'

'But I'm so out of practice with babies.'

Eliza patted her shoulder. 'And I haven't had any. I'm only good with new babies.'

Eliza couldn't become tangled up in Dulcie's plans. She needed to be free to escape from Jack as soon as Julie could find a replacement. 'I'll be there in the beginning, but if you get stuck you can ask Jack. He won't know either but he's great at finding people to help you.'

When Jack turned up that evening for his round, Eliza was busy and this time she didn't stop what she was doing. The situation between them was deteriorating and he needed to do something drastic.

Eliza had stayed in with a new mum to discuss settling techniques for her baby and after pausing, patiently waiting with them for a few minutes, Jack went on the round without her.

Later, Jack arrived at Eliza's house and she refused to open the door again. But this time he wasn't going to give up, or he wasn't going to before his pager went off and he was called away. When he finally made it back her lights were out.

Jack knew he'd blown it but this was ridiculous. She wouldn't escape him over the weekend, even if he had to break down the door.

CHAPTER ELEVEN

ELIZA'S friendship with Mary saved both of them from despair and Eliza dropped into a routine of visiting every evening after work for an hour or so.

They didn't discuss Jack because Eliza refused to, but Mary enjoyed hearing about the changes and admissions at the hospital. Eliza began to hope Mary might take up some part-time work to get her out of the house.

Nearly three weeks after the night with Jack, Eliza broached the subject. 'So, when do you want to return to work, Mary? Julie thinks she's found someone who is interested in part-time work here. I'll have been here eight weeks this time next week. That was my initial contract. You know I can finish up whenever you're ready to return to work.'

'I don't want you to go, Eliza. I admit I do think of going back to fill the horrible emptiness here, but then in the mornings I just can't seem to get myself motivated to even come in for a few hours.'

'Perhaps that's how we should start.' Eliza needed to leave despite the heartache of going. She'd wanted to go weeks ago but hadn't wanted to push Mary. She knew it was vital to make a fresh start with her own life and this time it would be different.

Mary saw that Eliza had drifted off into her own thoughts. Her eyes showed concern for her friend. 'How about you and Jack?'

Eliza glanced at Mary and then away again. 'What about Jack and I?'

Mary settled herself on the lounge beside Eliza and sighed for her friend's pain. 'Jack is alive for the first time in three years, though he seems a bit manic at the moment.'

Eliza shrugged. 'Jack and I don't have a relationship. I'm not going to be an emotional crutch for any man again.'

Eliza grimaced at Mary. 'The first time I had bad luck, the second started a pattern, and then there was Jack.' She shook her head vehemently. 'I don't think so, Mary.'

Mary tilted her head. 'But you and Jack are so well suited and could have a wonderful life together.'

Eliza avoided her eyes. 'I'm not staying around for the final episode.' She stared out the window at the mountains beyond the dam. 'The next man who asks me to marry him had better be damned sure I'm what he wants and have the church ready.' She grimaced at herself.

She drew a deep breath. 'That's why I think it's time for me to leave.' She looked across at her friend. 'But I will stay until Julie has found a relief for you.'

'Do you love Jack, Eliza?'

'No,' she lied. 'I can't afford to.' She tried to

avoid the memories that filled her mind when she thought of Jack. 'If I didn't have such a poor history I might conceivably risk my heart again, but this time I have to think of myself first. I'm worthy of a full man, one who wants to shout our love from the treetops and thinks of more than himself. I value myself now and I have you and Bellbrook to thank for that. It's because I'm strong I can walk away. I won't stay and hope he won't let me down.'

Mary nodded. 'I appreciate that, Eliza, and I understand your reluctance to be the rock again in a relationship. I just hope you both work it out. I promise I'll think of easing back to work.'

They went for a walk in the garden and when they returned Mary drew a deep breath. 'Could you stay and do the mornings for next week to see how I go? What if I started at lunch and finished when the night staff come in? That would be six hours each.'

Eliza nodded. Just the mornings. She'd miss Jack's evening rounds, Eliza thought as she forced a smile in Mary's direction. 'That sounds perfect, if it's not too much for you.'

On Friday night after work, unknown to Jack, Eliza had offered to drive an almost fully recovered Dulcie to Sydney to spend some time with her daughter, who was off the critical list.

The two women left early Saturday morning for the weekend, and Eliza dropped Dulcie off at the large city hospital where she had relative's accommodation for the night.

The sub-lease on Eliza's flat had ended and she needed to unpack her belongings again. And she'd decided it was time to face her mother.

Eliza pulled the crumpled business card out from the back of her father's photograph frame. She'd never been able to throw it away, although she'd almost forgotten where she'd hidden it. Eliza's mother had given it to her twelve years before at her father's graveside.

Mays of Mosman, Interior Decorator. Not

the sort of profession there would have been a call for from the isolation of her father's farm.

Eliza stared over the distance of time and instead of closing her mind she allowed the images from that day to wash through her memory. Surprisingly there was very little pain.

She could see her mother, elegant, dressed in a charcoal silk suit, stern-faced and determined to ensure Eliza didn't isolate herself from the world any longer.

Eliza remembered her own anger that her mother hadn't shed a tear and had accused her after the service of never having cared for her father.

Gwendolyn hadn't disputed Eliza's assumption. She had even said that leaving the valley had been the best thing she'd ever done, and that Eliza should leave, too.

Eliza had wanted to run and hide in the hills just as her father had done for the last ten years, but her mother had thwarted that from afar by selling the farm. Apart from the money

Eliza had needed to start nursing and live on campus, Gwendolyn had placed the money in trust for Eliza for her twenty-first birthday.

Eliza squeezed the business card between her fingers for a moment and then sighed. She could have a look, anyway.

When she pulled up outside her mother's shop she could see it was a prosperous business.

The understated chic and price tag on a tall, thin vase in the window confirmed Eliza would never have shopped there.

Eliza pushed open the door and browsed her way around the room past matching dinner sets and fine glassware, while the only customer completed her purchase.

'Hello, Eliza.' Her mother's voice was calm but the green eyes so much like Eliza's were startled.

'I wondered if you'd recognise me,' Eliza said, and moved up to the counter.

'What brings you here?' Gwendolyn asked, and Eliza wondered the same thing. Just what had she been hoping for or expecting from this woman she barely knew?

Gwendolyn glanced at the door as another customer entered and then looked back at Eliza.

'Please, don't go away. Stay and have lunch with me in a few minutes. I close the shop at lunchtime on Saturdays.'

It was almost as if she was glad she had come. Eliza nodded and stepped back to resume browsing while Gwendolyn attended to her customer.

Her mother looked older, which was extremely reasonable when she considered they hadn't seen each other for twelve years, but it was something Eliza hadn't factored in when she'd envisaged this meeting.

Eliza remembered when she'd visited Julie's mother with Julie once. The rapport between the two blond women, more like sisters than mother and daughter, had made Eliza realise the magnitude of her own loss.

As she surreptitiously watched Gwendolyn

smile at her customer, Eliza wondered if her mother felt she'd missed out, too. There was a certain sadness under the professional exterior and immaculate make-up. Eliza experienced the first thoughts of regret that she hadn't accepted her mother's overtures earlier.

As soon as the customer left, Gwendolyn turned the swinging plaque on the door to Closed. 'Where would you like to go?'

'It's your town.' Half of Eliza wanted to leave and the other didn't know what she wanted.

Gwendolyn knew what *she* wanted. 'Somewhere we can talk because I may not get to see you for another twelve years.'

'Are you saying that's my fault?' Eliza was beginning to think perhaps it might have been.

'I'd say the blame lies somewhere in the middle, but I'm glad you're here. I think of you a lot.'

Six words, but they changed many things. Her mother did think of her.

Eliza sighed. 'I guess I needed to grow up.

At least you sent Christmas and birthday cards. I've never sent anything.'

Her mother smiled ruefully and closed the door behind them. 'You never cash the cheques.'

Eliza felt her own lips tug. She'd never have imagined they could talk like this. 'I've a pile of them somewhere.'

'My accountant hates you.' Gwendolyn gestured to a low slung sports car. Eliza nodded and climbed in with her mother. The conversation stalled until they were seated in a secluded corner of a leafy restaurant.

'Why keep sending money?' She may not have cashed the cheques but Eliza had never been able to tear them up either.

'Because I have it and you'd have a return address if you ever wanted to find me. Because I hoped one day you'd forgive me for leaving you, because I never forgave myself.'

This was the crux of everything. This was what she had come for. 'Why did you leave and why did you leave me?'

'For a hundred reasons, but mostly because I didn't love your father. I left you with him because he was a better parent than I was and you adored him.'

Her voice was steady but Gwendolyn had a shine in her eyes that Eliza suspected was tears. 'I didn't want you to learn bad choices from me. I met and fell in lust with your father and should never have married him.'

She shrugged unhappily. 'I tried to make it right when you were born but as each year passed I became more bitter and frustrated by the closed lifestyle. When I realised I was going out more to stop myself going insane and the gossip started to circulate, I knew it was time to leave. I never regret leaving your father but I have always regretted leaving you.'

Not a good enough reason. 'I could never leave a child of mine.'

Gwendolyn looked across sardonically. 'Did you want to come with me?'

She had a point. 'No. I loved the farm and

the animals and Dad. I still love the country, but I seem to have acquired the skill of choosing men who lean on me to heal their emotional problems and then go on their way.'

'It's genetic,' her mother said dryly, and they both smiled.

This wasn't too bad. Eliza began to realise she should have made this move years ago. 'Why didn't you take me with you after the funeral?'

'You were eighteen. Legally a grown woman. I gave you my card and said come any time. I didn't think it would take twelve years.'

'That's not very maternal.'

'You told me you never wanted to hear from me again.'

Eliza remembered that.

Gwendolyn stretched her hand out and patted Eliza's fingers. 'How about we just start from here and see where we go? At least keep up with Christmas and birthdays and who knows? We may even come to enjoy each other's company.'

They smiled at each other and suddenly it didn't seem too far-fetched to have her mother somewhere in her life.

Sunday afternoon arrived and it was time to drive home. Except it wasn't home—it was where Jack belonged and she didn't.

Eliza collected Dulcie from her daughter's hospital and drove back to Bellbrook with a heavy heart. In the car she answered questions about the visit with her mother and Dulcie complacently congratulated herself on being responsible for their reunion.

Dulcie's daughter continued to improve and that visit had also been a success.

Monday saw the start of the shared week with Mary and Eliza began to pack her things.

As arranged, Eliza started work at seven and finished at one and Mary started at one and finished at seven.

By Wednesday Mary had settled back into the hospital and Eliza knew she was free to leave.

Eliza had stayed on at Dulcie's while the older woman settled into home life again. Now Dulcie could manage the cottage and the animals well. It was rewarding for Eliza to see her settled. She felt she'd achieved some good things during her time at Bellbrook.

Dulcie's daughter and granddaughter would come for an extended stay in two weeks time.

The sooner she could put Bellbrook behind her the better, but there was still Thursday and Friday to get through.

Jack was at a loss and beginning to panic that Eliza would leave and he'd lose her for ever. She wouldn't talk to him, or stay in the same room with him for longer than a few minutes. He'd written her two letters but both envelopes had been returned unopened. Finally he turned to Mary for help.

Mary stared at the frame on the dresser. The picture showed Amelia right after she was born, eyes wide open and inquisitive, and an emotional Mick in the background.

She shook her head at the tragedy. 'I don't know what I would have done without Eliza. I wouldn't have the beautiful photos and memories I have of Amelia, I know that. We were all so devastated and would never have arranged everything so well.'

Jack had trouble talking about Amelia's birth. Even though he'd known, and later tests had confirmed, that Amelia's heart and lungs had been incompatible with life, he'd felt there must have been something he could have done. Eliza's iron control and strength on that dreadful day still frightened him. 'She had enough distance to be able to do what those closer to you would have found difficult.'

Mary shook her head. 'That's not it at all, Jack. Do you believe that Eliza was distanced?' She shook her head and he got the feeling she was disappointed in him. 'You weren't there when I panicked at home, you didn't see the way she managed to get me to the hospital and into that bed and to the point, right at the end, when you and Mick arrived.

'She was the one who remembered to take photos that I'd sell my house to get back if I lost.'

Mary huffed at him in despair. 'Eliza didn't do all those things because she was safely distanced. She did them because she cared and she's strong and she's my friend.'

Mary stood up. 'Eliza is a very special woman. If you love her and let some stupid misunderstanding or fear of yours stand in the way, you will regret losing her for the rest of your life!'

Jack shook his head. 'I do regret it and I think I have lost her. I found something in Eliza that is beautiful and strong and I want that back. I thought she loved me the way I love her, but now there is a wall between us that I can't break.'

'Can't or won't, Jack.' Mary snorted. 'I heard that Eliza was seen leaving your house the night before Amelia was born.'

She stared mercilessly at him. 'Why was Eliza sneaking around? Why hadn't you taken her out to the most public restaurant and shown her off? Why isn't she wearing the biggest diamond you can buy? Eliza can't settle for half-measures or maybes. She's been let down too many times.' She shook her head. 'You know that!'

Jack spread his hands. 'I know.'

Mary wasn't going to go easy on him. 'Too many men have promised and not delivered, and now you've joined them. I don't know what happened between you two but you'd better sort it out as fast as you can.'

Jack didn't answer but Mary's words had him thinking. It hadn't just been a night, it had been a trial by fire and everything he'd dreamed that it could have been had come about that night. But the next day he'd blown it. Behaved as if what they'd shared had been nothing. Thrown her offer of comfort back in her face—as if she had been a stranger who couldn't help.

No wonder she'd changed. Frozen. And he couldn't get to her. She'd refused to talk to him, and had even threatened to leave the hospital immediately if he continued to harass her.

So he had left her alone, because if he waited he'd always got what he wanted, but Mary was right. He had to make plans or she would be gone. He had to believe she still loved him and that she was only scared he would let her down.

A glimmer of hope lightened his thoughts. There was only one way to prove his love to her but it would take a few days to organise. But he had plenty of helpers.

It started on Thursday. After days of Jack hounding Eliza to forgive him, she'd been driven to threaten she'd walk out. He'd finally left her alone but then something strange had started the next afternoon.

As she drove down the main street of town after work, people came out and waved at her.

Some older men on the corner clapped their hands and even the sour old lady from the tumble-down house next to the post office had waved and smiled.

Eliza couldn't figure it out unless they'd heard she was leaving and were saying goodbye.

She went to the post office for stamps for Dulcie, and when she entered, Mrs Green came around the counter and hugged her. 'I'm so pleased for you, dear. We all couldn't be happier.'

Eliza smiled and thanked her and wondered why they would be pleased she was leaving. It wasn't quite the sentiment she'd expected but, then, Bellbrook had bestowed a few of those moments on her during her time here.

When she'd gone to fill her car with fuel the garage proprietor had grinned from ear to ear and said he was 'right pleased you came here, we all are. You're a good girl'.

'Thank you.' Eliza paid for her fuel, smiled

and left with a puzzled look on her face. What was going on here?

Joe came out of the rural produce store, all smiles at seeing her, and hailed her from across the road. 'Great news, Matron,' he called and gave her the thumbs-up. Eliza smiled and waved back and swallowed the lump in her throat. She felt like leaving town now.

Then she ran into Carla of the first swimming incident. Carla held out her hand. 'I'm really happy for both of you.'

Eliza blinked. 'Both of who?'

'Why, you and Dr Jack getting married, of course.'

Eliza stared and backed away. She held her hands out in front of her. 'It's not true. Who told you that?'

'Everyone knows.'

'It's not true.'

Clearly Carla didn't believe her. 'Sure. But that's what I heard.'

Eliza fumbled with her key in the ignition

and nearly stalled the car as she did a three-point turn to get back to the hospital. She couldn't ask Jack, but Mary would surely know how this had all started.

As soon as Mary saw Eliza she swooped and hugged her.

'Congratulations. I'm so happy for you both.'

Eliza shook her head wildly and held up her hands again. 'You've heard it, too. It's not true.'

'It must be. Jack told me.'

'He can't do that. He can't just tell everyone we're getting married and expect me to fall in with his plans.'

'The church is booked for ten a.m. on Saturday.'

'What?' Eliza's voice carried shrilly down the hallway and she clapped her hand over her mouth at the echo. Eliza looked around but there wasn't anyone else in the corridor. Her head was spinning.

'I'm sorry, but this is ridiculous.'

'He's invited your mother.'

'What?' Her voice was quieter but still shrill.

Eliza looked wildly from side to side. 'I have to find Jack. Where is he?'

'He had to go to Armidale to see the administrators at the hospital. He's arranging time off for your honeymoon.'

'I'm not having a honeymoon. I'm not having a wedding. Does he expect me to meekly turn up at the right time? How can a man who didn't want me to tell anyone do this?'

'I guess it depends how desperate he is.' Mary's words hung in the air and Eliza started to believe Jack really had created this fiasco. She'd kill him.

Eliza turned around slowly, and as Mary watched her sympathetically, she walked away. Was Jack that desperate to marry her?

CHAPTER TWELVE

JACK rang the doorbell at Dulcie's early that evening. 'Mary said you wanted to see me.' Jack was dressed in black trousers and a white shirt open at the neck, and he carried a yellow rose. Eliza had never seen him look so handsome. The pain sliced through her at what might have been, but she couldn't trust him.

She should have left days ago. It was too cruel.

'Let's walk in the garden.' Eliza couldn't meet his eyes and she hurried past him on the steps to get ahead. He caught up to her and there was a strange expression in his eyes that didn't fit any of the scenarios she'd dreamed up in her mind. She felt more confused than ever.

Eliza stopped and faced him. 'I'm not marrying you!' she said baldly. 'You can't just get married. You have to have a licence and banns read in church and invitations and things.'

He shrugged but that soft smile stayed on his lips. 'You met all those criteria before and you didn't get married. This time you will marry but without the banns. The application for a licence you need to sign tonight.'

Eliza shook her head. 'I'm not signing any-thing!'

Here was his angry fairy from the first time he'd seen her. Her green eyes were flashing and she stood with her hands on her hips and glared at him, although there was a shadow of pain at the backs of her eyes. He'd caused that and he felt his heart squeeze in regret. She came up to his shoulder and he loved her so much it hurt to breathe—just like the first time he'd seen her.

There had to be a way to get through to her. His voice softened. Where had she been at her weakest? 'What about if I kissed you? Would you marry me then?'

Jack took Eliza's hand and she shuddered at the feeling of his fingers around hers. He stared down into her eyes. 'I know you didn't believe me when I said I fell in love with you, Eliza. But it's true.

'I want to change your mind. I ask you to give me one more chance at winning the woman I will love for ever. Be my bride, here, on Saturday, in front of the whole town and all your friends. They all think we belong together, as I do, and I've asked them to help me sway you. Will you let it happen? Marry me, Eliza, please.'

She shook her head and her eyes filled with tears.

Jack went on ignoring her denial. 'We could start the rest of out lives together with no more misunderstandings between us and no more delay.'

Eliza could taste the tears and her head was so confused and unsure and terrified that she turned her back on him to get away to think about this, but he still had hold of her hand. Her arms stretched but he didn't let go and she turned back to face him.

He opened her palm and pressed a little ring with an enormous emerald into her palm. 'Will you wear my ring?'

It was all too much to grasp. How could this happen? She shook her head and before she could make any sense he took her chin in his other hand and settled his lips on hers.

Slowly, as if seeing through mist, floating like a piece of driftwood in Dulcie's creek, she finally glimpsed the sunlight shining on paradise. Eliza began to wonder if she'd been wrong.

Jack against her, his mouth and his breath entwined with hers, murmuring he loved her. When the kiss deepened she sank against him. The feel, the taste, the scent and the strength of him surrounded her, and his arms around her kept her safe. He felt so strong and sure and Jack-like, so sure for both of them, she could feel her resistance dissipate.

When he stepped back she stared at him and took a deep breath.

This risked everything. 'Maybe you should have kissed me earlier.' She smiled whimsically. 'I love you, too, but if you hurt me, I don't think I will survive.'

He hugged her. 'Neither would I. I'm sorry I took so long to kiss you. When I realised how stupid I'd been on our first morning together I could have kicked myself, but it wasn't because I wasn't proud and honoured to have you in my heart. I had ghosts to lay, and I'm sorry I hurt you.'

He tilted her chin up towards him with his finger. 'You haven't said yes yet.'

'Yes,' she said faintly, and at the wonder in her face he kissed her again.

'It's OK. Now I have you. I can be a simple man, too, when I have all I want. Are you sure you can live at Bellbrook for ever?'

'I could live in Antarctica for ever if I was with you but, yes, I've grown to love Bellbrook and I have good friends here, too.'

'I'm not asking you to be isolated. We'll do dashes to Sydney and paint the town red before coming back to our home. I've learnt I'm not irreplaceable and we need to get away even if just to appreciate how great it is here.'

'I think you're irreplaceable but that sounds wonderful.'

They left Dulcie's and drove to his house where they spent hours talking and making love. Late in the evening Jack rose and brought back a platter of food which they devoured sitting up in bed.

'We are going to have the most beautiful wedding in the world but now we need to drive to town to see the minister. I've run out of excuses and he's a little suspicious of my fiancée's consent.'

'As he should be! Imagine everyone in town knowing I was getting married this Saturday except me. They applauded me on street corners and I thought they were glad I was going.'

Jack laughed, which was very unsporting of him. 'Forgive me.'

'Maybe.' She pretended to glare again and he couldn't help kissing her.

Later, after they'd satisfied the minister that they were truly in love, and deserved to be married, they left the tiny church. Jack took her home again to his house on the hill and they sat on the swing seat and held hands and watched the stars.

'There is so much to do.' Suddenly Eliza felt swamped with the enormity of an imminent wedding.

Jack smiled and kissed her. 'Tomorrow your mother is coming and she's ordered a truckful of bridal gowns for you to choose from. She mentioned beauticians and a hairstylist so I doubt you'll have much time for me after tonight. From my conversations with her, she's dying to do something for you and I doubt you'll need to lift a finger. Between Gwendolyn and the ladies of Bellbrook, everything will be perfect.'

Everything was happening too fast but Eliza wasn't complaining this time. She'd sit back and enjoy the ride. 'How many conversations have you had with my mother?'

'Enough to know she will be a part of our lives in the future—as she should be.' He leant across and kissed her to change the subject. 'Did I tell you I love you?'

Three days later the most beautiful wedding in the world began.

The wedding march thundered out of the huge old organ that took up most of one wall of the tiny church. The music was enthusiastically rendered by one of the ladies from the hospital auxiliary in an equally loud hat.

Magnificent floral arrangements had been assembled from gardens all over the valley by the members of the Country Women's

Association and the air was heavy with floral scent and a few satiated bees.

The minister, who had christened Jack and his family for decades, had prepared a resounding homily on the evils of gossip and the strength of love.

All heads turned as Eliza entered the church with her hand resting in the crook of Keith's arm. The old farmer wore his Sunday suit and his wrinkled face beamed with pride at the beautiful young woman beside him.

Eliza floated down the aisle towards her husband-to-be who waited with his hand outstretched. On his lapel he wore a tiny pair of crystal wings.

A ripple of satisfaction flowed around the church as friends and family saw the look of adoration on Jack's face and the bride's mother unobtrusively dabbed her damp eyes.

When the bride and groom stood together in front of the altar and repeated their vows, the solemn words were so clear and firm that they carried easily to the furthest pew.

Here were no second thoughts, no doubt that they would love each other always, no hesitation in uniting in holy matrimony.

Afterwards, to an even louder swell of triumphant music, Dr and Mrs Jack Dancer greeted their family and friends—and there were so many of them!

Later that night, finally alone in a luxurious mountain retreat near Byron Bay, Jack held his fairy queen tight against his heart. The spell around them shimmered in the moonlight and he silently thanked his family and friends for bringing his heart to him.

'I love you,' he murmured to Eliza as she slept beside him. In her sleep, her hand crept into his, and he held her close all through the night.